Brief ENCOUNTERS

FYODOR DOSTOEVSKY

Born in Moscow in 1821, Fyodor Mikhaylovich Dostoevsky is regarded as one of the most influential writers who ever lived. After being exiled and imprisoned in Siberia, experiencing near-execution and losing much of his wealth and dignity to a gambling addiction, Dostoevsky went on to write some of the greatest and most penetrating novels of the modern era – including *The Idiot*, *Crime and Punishment* and *The Brothers Karamazov*. He died in 1881 in St Petersburg.

ALSO BY FYODOR DOSTOEVSKY

The Brothers Karamazov

Crime and Punishment

Demons

The Devils

The Gambler

The Idiot

Notes from Underground

FYODOR DOSTOEVSKY

A GENTLE SPIRIT
and
A FAINT HEART

Two Novellas

Translated from the Russian by
Constance Garnett

Brief ENCOUNTERS

VINTAGE CLASSICS

1 3 5 7 9 10 8 6 4 2

Vintage Classics is part of the Penguin Random House group of companies

Vintage, Penguin Random House UK, One Embassy Gardens,
8 Viaduct Gardens, London SW11 7BW

penguin.co.uk/vintage-classics
global.penguinrandomhouse.com

This edition published in Vintage Classics in 2026
A Gentle Spirit first published in Russia in 1876
A Faint Heart first published in Russia in 1848

The moral right of the author has been asserted

Typeset in 12.6/15pt Bembo Book MT Pro by Six Red Marbles UK, Thetford, Norfolk
Printed and bound in Great Britain by Clays Ltd, Elcograf S.p.A.

The authorised representative in the EEA is Penguin Random House Ireland,
Morrison Chambers, 32 Nassau Street, Dublin D02 YH68

A CIP catalogue record for this book is available from the British Library

ISBN 9781529981483

Penguin Random House is committed to a sustainable future
for our business, our readers and our planet. This book is made
from Forest Stewardship Council® certified paper.

A Gentle Spirit

PART ONE

CHAPTER I

Who I Was and Who She Was

Oh, while she is still here, it is still all right; I go up and look at her every minute; but tomorrow they will take her away — and how shall I be left alone? Now she is on the table in the drawing-room, they put two card tables together, the coffin will be here tomorrow — white, pure white 'gros de Naples' — but that's not it . . .

I keep walking about, trying to explain it to myself. I have been trying for the last six hours to get it clear, but still I can't think of it all as a whole.

The fact is I walk to and fro, and to and fro.

This is how it was. I will simply tell it in order. (Order!)

Gentlemen, I am far from being a literary man and you will see that; but no matter, I'll tell it as I understand it myself. The horror of it for me is that I understand it all!

It was, if you care to know, that is to take it from the beginning, that she used to come to me simply to pawn things, to pay for advertising in the VOICE to the effect that a governess was quite willing to travel, to give lessons at home, and so on, and so on. That was at the very beginning, and I, of course, made no difference between her and the others: 'She comes,' I thought, 'like anyone else,' and so on.

But afterwards I began to see a difference. She was such a slender, fair little thing, rather tall, always a little awkward with me, as though embarrassed (I fancy she was the same with all strangers, and in her eyes, of course, I was exactly like anybody else — that is, not as a pawn-broker but as a man).

As soon as she received the money she would turn round at once and go away. And always in silence. Other women argue so, entreat, haggle for me to give them more; this one did not ask for more . . .

I believe I am muddling it up.

Yes; I was struck first of all by the things she brought: poor little silver gilt earrings, a trashy little locket, things not worth sixpence. She knew herself that they were worth next to nothing, but I could see from her face that they were treasures to her, and I found out afterwards as a fact that they were all that was left her belonging to her father and mother.

Only once I allowed myself to scoff at her things. You see I never allow myself to behave like that. I keep up a gentlemanly tone with my clients: few words, politeness and severity. 'Severity, severity!'

But once she ventured to bring her last rag, that is, literally the remains of an old hareskin jacket, and I could not resist saying something by way of a joke. My goodness! how she flared up! Her eyes were large, blue and dreamy but — how they blazed. But she did not drop one word; picking up her 'rags' she walked out.

It was then for the first time I noticed her particularly, and thought something of the kind about her — that is, something of a particular kind. Yes, I remember another impression — that is, if you will have it, perhaps the chief impression, that summed up everything. It was that she was terribly young, so young that she looked just fourteen. And yet she was within three months of sixteen. I didn't mean that, though, that wasn't what summed it all up. Next day she came again. I found out later that she had been to Dobranravov's and to Mozer's with that jacket, but they take nothing but gold and would have nothing to say to it. I once took some stones from her (rubbishy little ones) and, thinking it over afterwards, I wondered: I, too, only lend on gold and silver, yet from her I accepted stones. That was my second thought about her then; that I remember. That time, that is when she came from Mozer's, she brought an amber cigar-holder. It was a connoisseur's article, not bad, but again, of no value to us, because we only deal in gold. As it was the day after her 'mutiny', I received her sternly. Sternness with me takes the form of dryness. As I gave her two roubles, however, I could not resist saying, with a certain irritation, 'I only do it for you, of course; Mozer wouldn't take such a thing.'

The word 'for you' I emphasised particularly, and with a particular implication.

I was spiteful. She flushed up again when she heard that 'for you', but she did not say a word, she did not refuse the money, she took it — that is poverty! But how hotly she flushed! I saw I had stung her. And when she had gone out, I suddenly asked myself whether my triumph over her was worth two roubles. He! He!! He!!! I remember I put that question to myself twice over, 'was is worth it? was it worth it?'

And, laughing, I inwardly answered it in the affirmative. And I felt very much elated. But that was not an evil feeling; I said it with design, with a motive; I wanted to test her, because certain ideas with regard to her had suddenly come into my mind. That was the third thing I thought particularly about her . . . Well, it was from that time it all began. Of course, I tried at once to find out all her circumstances indirectly, and awaited her coming with a special impatience. I had a presentiment that she would come soon. When she came, I entered into affable conversation with her, speaking with unusual politeness. I have not been badly brought up and have manners. H'm. It was then I guessed that she was soft-hearted and gentle.

The gentle and soft-hearted do not resist long, and though they are by no means very ready to reveal themselves, they do not know how to escape from a conversation; they are niggardly in their answers, but they do answer, and the more readily the longer you go on. Only, on your side you must not flag, if you want them to talk. I need hardly say that she did not explain anything to me then. About the Voice and all that I found out afterwards. She was at that time spending her last farthing on advertising, haughtily at first, of course. 'A governess prepared to travel and will send terms on application,' but, later on: 'willing to do anything, to teach, to be a companion, to be a housekeeper, to wait on an invalid, plain sewing, and so on, and so on', the usual thing! Of course, all this was added to the advertisement a bit at a time and finally, when she was reduced to despair, it came to: 'without salary in return for board.' No, she could not find a situation. I made up my mind then to test her for the last time. I suddenly took up the Voice of the day and showed her an advertisement. 'A young person, without friends and relations, seeks a situation as a governess to young children, preferably in the family of a middle-aged widower. Might be a comfort in the home.'

'Look here how this lady has advertised this morning, and by the evening she will certainly have found a situation. That's the way to advertise.'

Again she flushed crimson and her eyes blazed, she turned round and went straight out. I was very much pleased, though by that time I felt sure of everything and had no apprehensions; nobody will take her cigar-holders, I thought. Besides, she has got rid of them all. And so it was, two days later, she came in again, such a pale little creature, all agitation — I saw that something had happened to her at home, and something really had. I will explain directly what had happened, but now I only want to recall how I did something chic, and rose in her opinion. I suddenly decided to do it. The fact is she was pawning the ikon (she had brought herself to pawn it!) . . . Ah! listen! listen! This is the beginning now, I've been in a muddle. You see I want to recall all this, every detail, every little point. I want to bring them all together and look at them as a whole and — I cannot . . . It's these little things, these little things . . . It was an ikon of the Madonna. A Madonna with the Babe, and old-fashioned, homely one, and the setting was silver gilt, worth — well, six roubles perhaps. I could see the ikon was precious to her; she was pawning it whole, not taking it out of the setting. I said to her—

'You had better take it out of the setting, and take the ikon home; for it's not the thing to pawn.'

'Why, are you forbidden to take them?'

'No, it's not that we are forbidden, but you might, perhaps, yourself . . .'

'Well, take it out.'

'I tell you what. I will not take it out, but I'll set it here in the shrine with the other ikons,' I said, on reflection. 'Under the little lamp' (I always had the lamp burning as soon as the shop was opened), 'and you simply take ten roubles.'

'Don't give me ten roubles. I only want five; I shall certainly redeem it.'

'You don't want ten? The ikon's worth it,' I added noticing that her eyes flashed again.

She was silent. I brought out five roubles.

'Don't despise anyone; I've been in such straits myself; and worse too, and that you see me here in this business . . . is owing to what I've been through in the past . . .'

'You're revenging yourself on the world? Yes?' she interrupted suddenly with rather sarcastic mockery, which, however, was to a great extent innocent (that is, it was general, because certainly at that time she did not distinguish me from others, so that she said it almost without malice).

'Aha,' thought I; 'so that's what you're like. You've got character; you belong to the new movement.'

'You see!' I remarked at once, half-jestingly,

half-mysteriously, 'I am part of that part of the Whole that seeks to do ill, but does good . . .'

Quickly and with great curiosity, in which, however, there was something very childlike, she looked at me.

'Stay . . . what's that idea? Where does it come from? I've heard it somewhere . . .'

'Don't rack your brains. In those words Mephistopheles introduces himself to Faust. Have you read Faust?'

'Not . . . not attentively.'

'That is, you have not read it at all. You must read it. But I see an ironical look in your face again. Please don't imagine that I've so little taste as to try to use Mephistopheles to commend myself to you and grace the role of pawnbroker. A pawnbroker will still be a pawnbroker. We know.'

'You're so strange . . . I didn't mean to say anything of that sort.'

She meant to say: 'I didn't expect to find you were an educated man'; but she didn't say it; I knew, though, that she thought that. I had pleased her very much.

'You see,' I observed, 'one may do good in any calling – I'm not speaking of myself, of course. Let us grant that I'm doing nothing but harm, yet . . .'

'Of course, one can do good in every position,' she said, glancing at me with a rapid, profound look. 'Yes, in any position,' she added suddenly.

Oh, I remember, I remember all those moments! And I want to add, too, that when such young creatures, such sweet young creatures want to say something so clever and profound, they show at once so truthfully and naively in their faces, 'Here I am saying something clever and profound now' – and that is not from vanity, as it is with any one like me, but one sees that she appreciates it awfully herself, and believes in it, and thinks a lot of it, and imagines that you think a lot of all that, just as she does. Oh, truthfulness! it's by that they conquer us. How exquisite it was in her!

I remember it, I have forgotten nothing! As soon as she had gone, I made up my mind. That same day I made my last investigations and found out every detail of her position at the moment; every detail of her past I had learned already from Lukerya, at that time a servant in the family, whom I had bribed a few days before. This position was so awful that I can't understand how she could laugh as she had done that day and feel interest in the words of Mephistopheles, when she was in such horrible straits. But – that's youth! That is just what I thought about her at the time with pride and joy; for, you know, there's a greatness of soul in it – to be able to say, 'Though I am on the edge of the abyss, yet Goethe's grand words are radiant with light.' Youth always has some greatness of soul, if its only a spark and that distorted. Though it's of her I am speaking, of her alone. And, above all, I looked upon her then as mine and did not doubt of my power. You know, that's a voluptuous idea when you feel no doubt of it.

But what is the matter with me? If I go on like this, when shall I put it all together and look at it as a whole. I must make haste, make haste – that is not what matters, oh, my God!

CHAPTER 2

The Offer of Marriage

The 'details' I learned about her I will tell in one word: her father and mother were dead, they had died three years before, and she had been left with two disreputable aunts: though it is saying too little to call them disreputable. One aunt was a widow with a large family (six children, one smaller than another), the other a horrid old maid. Both were horrid. Her father was in the service, but only as a copying clerk, and was only a gentleman by courtesy; in fact, everything was in my favour. I came as though from a higher world; I was anyway a retired lieutenant of a brilliant regiment, a gentleman by birth, independent and all the rest of it, and as for my pawnbroker's shop, her aunts could only have looked on that with respect. She had been living in slavery at her aunts' for those three years: yet she had managed to pass an examination somewhere – she managed to pass it, she wrung the time for it, weighed down as a she was by the pitiless burden of daily drudgery, and that proved something in the way of striving for what was higher and better on her part! Why, what made me want to marry her? Never mind me, though; of that later on . . . As though that mattered! – She taught her aunt's children; she made their clothes; and towards the end not only washed the clothes, but with her weak chest even scrubbed the floors. To put it plainly, they used to beat her, and taunt her with eating their bread. It ended by their scheming to sell her. Tfoo! I omit the filthy details. She told me all about it afterwards.

All this had been watched for a whole year by a neighbour, a fat shopkeeper, and not a humble one but the owner of two grocer's shops. He had ill-treated two wives and now he was looking for a third, and so he cast his eye on her. 'She's a quiet one,' he thought; 'she's grown up in poverty, and I am marrying for the sake of my motherless children.' He really had children. He began trying to make the match and negotiating with the aunts. He was fifty years old, besides. She was aghast with horror. It was then she began coming so often to me to advertise in the Voice. At last she began begging the aunts to give her just a little time to think it over. They granted her that little time, but would not let her have more; they were always at her: 'We don't know where to turn to find food for ourselves, without an extra mouth to feed.'

I had found all this out already, and the same day, after what had happened in the morning, I made up my mind. That evening the shopkeeper came, bringing with him a pound of sweets from the shop; she was sitting with him, and I called Lukerya out of the kitchen and told her to go and whisper to her that I was at the gate and wanted to say something to her without delay. I felt pleased with myself. And altogether I felt awfully pleased all that day.

On the spot, at the gate, in the presence of Lukerya, before she had recovered from her amazement at my sending for her, I informed her that I should look upon it as an honour and happiness . . . telling her, in the next place, not to be surprised at the manner of my declaration and at my speaking at the gate, saying that I was a straight-forward man and had learned the position of affairs. And I was not lying when I said I was straightforward. Well, hang it all. I did not only speak with propriety – that is, showing I was a man of decent breeding, but I spoke with originality and that was the chief thing. After all, is there any harm in admitting it? I want to judge myself and am judging myself. I must speak pro and contra, and I do. I remembered afterwards with enjoyment, though it was stupid, that I frankly declared, without the least embar-rassment, that, in the first place, I was not particularly talented, not particularly intelligent, not particularly good-natured, rather a cheap egoist (I remember that expression, I thought of it on the way and was pleased with it) and that very probably there was a great deal that was disagreeable in me in other respects. All this was said with a special sort of pride – we all know how that sort of thing is said. Of course, I had good taste enough not to proceed to enlarge on my virtues after honourably enu-merating my defects, not to say 'to make up for that I have this and that and the other.' I saw that she was still horrible frightened I purposely exaggerated. I told her straight out that she would have enough to eat, but that fine clothes, theatres, balls – she would have none of, at any rate not till later on, when I had attained my object. This severe tone was a positive delight to me. I added as

cursorily as possible, that in adopting such a calling —
that is, in keeping a pawnbroker's shop, I had one object,
hinting there was a special circumstance . . . but I really
had a right to say so: I really had such an aim and there
really was such a circumstance. Wait a minute, gentlemen; I have always been the first to hate this pawnbroking business, but in reality, though it is absurd to talk
about oneself in such mysterious phrases, yet, you know,
I was 'revenging myself on society,' I really was, I was,
I was! So that her gibe that morning at the idea of my
revenging myself was unjust. That is, do you see, if I had
said to her straight out in words: 'yes, I am revenging
myself on society,' she would have laughed as she did
that morning, and it would, in fact have been absurd.
But by indirect hints, but dropping mysterious phrases,
it appeared that it was possible to work upon her im-
agination. Besides, I had no fears then: I knew that the fat
shopkeeper was anyway more repulsive to her than I was,
and that I, standing at the gate, had appeared as a deliv-
erer. I understood that, of course. Oh, what is base a man
understands particularly well! But was it base? How can
a man judge? Didn't I love her even then?

Wait a bit: of course, I didn't breathe a word to her of
doing her a benefit; the opposite, oh, quite the opposite;
I made out that it was I that would be under an obli-
gation to her, not she to me. Indeed, I said as much — I
couldn't resist saying it — and it sounded stupid, perhaps,
for I noticed a shade flit across her face. But altogether I
won the day completely. Wait a bit, if I am to recall all
that vileness, then I will tell of that worst beastliness. As
I stood there what was stirring in my mind was, 'You

are tall, a good figure, educated and — speaking without conceit — good-looking.' That is what was at work in my mind. I need hardly say that, on the spot, out there at the gate she said 'yes.' But . . . but I ought to add: that out there by the gate she thought a long time before she said 'yes.' She pondered for so long that I said to her, 'Well?' — and could not even refrain from asking it with a certain swagger.

'Wait a little. I'm thinking.'

And her little face was so serious, so serious that even then I might have read it! And I was mortified: 'Can she be choosing between me and the grocer!' I thought. Oh, I did not understand then! I did not understand anything, anything, then! I did not understand till today! I remember Lukerya ran after me as I was going away, stopped me on the road and said, breathlessly: 'God will reward you, sir, for taking our dear young lady; only don't speak of that to her — she's proud.'

Proud, is she! 'I like proud people,' I thought. Proud people are particularly nice when . . . well, when one has no doubt of one's power over them, eh? Oh, base, tactless man! Oh, how pleased I was! You know, when she was standing there at the gate, hesitating whether to say 'yes' to me, and I was wondering at it, you know, she may have had some such thought as this: 'If it is to be misery either way, isn't it best to choose the very worst' — that is, let the fat grocer beat her to death when he was drunk! Eh! what do you think, could there have been a thought like that?

And, indeed, I don't understand it now, I don't understand it at all, even now. I have only just said that she may have had that thought: of two evils choose the worst — that is the grocer. But which was the worst for her then — the grocer or I? The grocer or the pawnbroker who quoted Goethe? That's another question! What a question! And even that you don't understand: the answer is lying on the table and you call it a question! Never mind me, though. It's not a question of me at all . . . and, by the way, what is there left for me now — whether it's a question of me or whether it is not? That's what I am utterly unable to answer. I had better go to bed. My head aches . . .

CHAPTER 3

The Noblest of Men, Though
I Don't Believe It Myself

I could not sleep. And how should I? There is a pulse throbbing in my head. One longs to master it all, all that degradation. Oh, the degradation! Oh, what degradation I dragged her out of then! Of course, she must have realised that, she must have appreciated my action! I was pleased, too, by various thoughts – for instance, the reflection that I was forty-one and she was only sixteen. That fascinated me, that feeling of inequality was very sweet, was very sweet.

I wanted, for instance, to have a wedding a l'anglaise, that is only the two of us, with just the two necessary witnesses, one of them Lukerya, and from the wedding straight to the train to Moscow (I happened to have business there, by the way), and then a fortnight at the hotel. She opposed it, she would not have it, and I had to visit her aunts and treat them with respect as though they were relations from whom I was taking her. I gave way, and all befitting respect was paid the aunts. I even made the creatures a present of a hundred roubles each and promised them more – not telling her anything about it, of course, that I might not make her feel humiliated by the lowness of her surroundings. The aunts were as soft as silk at once. There was a wrangle about the trousseau too; she had nothing, almost literally, but she did not want to have anything. I succeeded in proving to her, though, that she must have something, and I made up the trousseau, for who would have given her anything? But there, enough of me. I did, however, succeed in communicating some of my ideas to her then, so that she knew them anyway. I was in too great a hurry, perhaps. The best of it was that, from the very beginning, she rushed to meet me with love, greeted me with rapture, when I went to see her in the evening, told me in her chatter (the enchanting chatter of innocence) all about her childhood and girlhood, her old home, her father and mother. But I poured cold water upon all that at once. That was my idea. I met her enthusiasm with silence, friendly silence, of course . . . but, all the same, she could quickly see that we were different and that I was – an enigma. And being an enigma was what I made a point of most of all! Why, it was just for the sake of being an enigma, perhaps – that I have been guilty of all this stupidity. The first thing was sternness – it was with an air of sternness that I took her into my house. In fact, as I went about then feeling satisfied, I framed a complete system. Oh, it came of itself without any effort. And it could not have been otherwise. I was bound to create that system owing to one inevitable fact – why should I libel myself indeed! The system was a genuine one. Yes, listen; if you must judge a man, better judge him knowing all about it . . . listen.

How am I to begin this, for it is very difficult. When you begin to justify yourself – then it is difficult. You see, for instance, young people despise money – I made money of importance at once; I laid special stress on money. And laid such stress on it that she became more and more silent. She opened her eyes wide, listened, gazed and said nothing. You see, the young are heroic, that is the good among them are heroic and impulsive, but they have little tolerance; if the least thing is not quite right they are full of contempt. And I wanted breadth, I wanted to instil breadth into her very heart, to make it part of her inmost feeling, did I not? I'll take a trivial example: how should I explain my pawnbroker's shop to a character like that? Of course, I did not speak of it directly, or it would have appeared that I was apologising, and I, so to speak, worked it through with pride, I almost spoke without words, and I am masterly at speaking without words. All my life I have spoken without words, and I have passed through whole tragedies on my own account without words. Why, I, too, have been unhappy! I was abandoned by everyone, abandoned and forgotten, and no one, no one knew it! And all at once this sixteen-year-old girl picked up details about me from vulgar people and thought she knew all about me, and, meanwhile, what was precious remained hidden in this heart! I went on being silent, with her especially I was silent, with her especially, right up to yesterday – why was I silent? Because I was proud. I wanted her to find out for herself, without my help, and not from the tales of low people; I wanted her to divine of herself what manner of man I was and to understand me! Taking her into my house I wanted all her respect, I wanted her to be standing before me in homage for the sake of my sufferings – and I deserved it. Oh, I have always been proud, I always wanted all or nothing! You see it was just because I am not one who will accept half a happiness, but always wanted all, that I was forced to act like that then: it was as much as to say, 'See into me for yourself and appreciate me!' For you must see that if I had begun explaining myself to her and prompting her, ingratiating myself and asking for her respect – it would have been as good as asking for charity . . . But . . . but why am I talking of that!

Stupid, stupid, stupid, stupid! I explained to her then, in two words, directly, ruthlessly (and I emphasise the fact that it was ruthlessly) that the heroism of youth was charming, but – not worth a farthing. Why not? Because it costs them so little, because it is not gained through life; it is, so to say, merely 'first impressions of existence,' but just let us see you at work! Cheap heroism is always easy, and even to sacrifice life is easy too; because it is only a case of hot blood and an overflow of energy, and there is such a longing for what is beautiful! No, take the deed of heroism that is laborious, obscure, without noise or flourish, slandered, in which there is a great deal of sacrifice and not one grain of glory – in which you, a splendid man, are made to look like a scoundrel before every one, though you might be the most honest man in the world – you try that sort of heroism and you'll soon give it up! While I – have been bearing the burden of that all my life. At first she argued – ough, how she argued – but afterwards she began to be silent, completely silent, in fact, only opened her eyes wide as she listened, such big, big eyes, so attentive. And . . . and what is more, I suddenly saw a smile, mistrustful, silent, an evil smile. Well, it was with that smile on her face I brought her into my house. It is true that she had nowhere to go.

CHAPTER 4

Plans and Plans

Which of us began it first?

Neither. It began of itself from the very first. I have said that with sternness I brought her into the house. From the first step, however, I softened it. Before she was married it was explained to her that she would have to take pledges and pay out money, and she said nothing at the time (note that). What is more, she set to work with positive zeal. Well, of course, my lodging, my furniture all remained as before. My lodging consisted of two rooms, a large room from which the shop was partitioned off, and a second one, also large, our living room and bedroom. My furniture is scanty: even her aunts had better things. My shrine of ikons with the lamp was in the outer room where the shop is; in the inner room my bookcase with a few books in and a trunk of which I keep the key; married I told her that one rouble a day and not more, was to be spent on our board – that is, on food for me, her and Lukerya whom I had enticed to come to us. 'I must have thirty thousand in three years,' said I, 'and we can't save the money if we spend more.' She fell in with this, but I raised the sum by thirty kopecks a day. It was the same with the theatre. I told her before marriage that she would not go to the theatre, and yet I decided once a month to go to the theatre, and in a decent way, to the stalls. We went together. We went three times and saw The Hunt after Happiness, and Singing Birds, I believe. (Oh, what does it matter!) We went in silence and in silence we returned. Why, why, from the very beginning, did we take to being silent? From the very first, you know, we had no quarrels, but always the same silence. She was always, I remember, watching me stealthily in those days; as soon as I noticed it I became more silent than before. It is true that it was I insisted on the silence, not she. On her part there were one or two outbursts, she rushed to embrace me; but as these outbursts were hysterical, painful, and I wanted secure happiness, with respect from her, I received them coldly. And indeed, I was right; each time the outburst was followed next day by a quarrel.

Though, again, there were no quarrels, but there was silence and — and on her side a more and more defiant air. 'Rebellion and independence,' that's what it was, only she didn't know how to show it. Yes, that gentle creature was becoming more and more defiant. Would you believe it, I was becoming revolting to her? I learned that. And there could be no doubt that she was moved to frenzy at times. Think, for instance, of her beginning to sniff at our poverty, after her coming from such sordidness and destitution — from scrubbing the floors! You see, there was no poverty; there was frugality, but there was abundance of what was necessary, of linen, for instance, and the greatest cleanliness. I always used to dream that cleanliness in a husband attracts a wife. It was not our poverty she was scornful of, but my supposed miserliness in the housekeeping: 'he has his objects,' she seemed to say, 'he is showing his strength of will.' She suddenly refused to go to the theatre. And more and more often an ironical look . . . And I was more silent, more and more silent.

I could not begin justifying myself, could I? What was at the bottom of all this was the pawnbroking business. Allow me, I knew that a woman, above all at sixteen, must be in complete subordination to a man. Women have no originality. That — that is an axiom; even now, even now, for me it is an axiom! What does it prove that she is lying there in the outer room? Truth is truth, and even Mill is no use against it! And a woman who loves, oh, a woman who loves idealises even the vices, even the villainies of the man she loves. He would not himself even succeed in finding such justification for his villainies as she will find for him. That is generous but not original. It is the lack of originality alone that has been the ruin of women. And, I repeat, what is the use of your point to that table? Why, what is there original in her being on that table? O – O – Oh!

Listen. I was convinced of her love at that time. Why, she used to throw herself on my neck in those days. She loved me; that is, more accurately, she wanted to love. Yes, that's just what it was, she wanted to love; she was trying to love. And the point was that in this case there were no villainies for which she had to find justification. You will say, I'm a pawnbroker; and everyone says the same. But what if I am a pawnbroker? It follows that there must be reasons since the most generous of men had become a pawnbroker. You see, gentlemen, there are ideas . . . that is, if one expresses some ideas, utters them in words, the effect is very stupid. The effect is to make one ashamed. For what reason? For no reason. Because we are all wretched creatures and cannot hear the truth, or I do not know why. I said just now, 'the most generous of men' – that is absurd, and yet that is how it was. It's the truth, that is, the absolute, absolute truth! Yes, I had the right to want to make myself secure and open that pawnbroker's shop: 'You have rejected me, you – people, I mean – you have cast me out with contemptuous silence. My passionate yearning towards you you have met with insult all my life. Now I have the right to put up a wall against you, to save up that thirty thousand roubles and end my life somewhere in the Crimea, on the south coast, among the mountains and vineyards, on my own estate bought with that thirty thousand, and above everything, far away from you all, living without malice against you, with an ideal in my soul, with a beloved woman at my heart, and a family, if God sends one, and – helping the inhabitants all around.'

Of course, it is quite right that I say this to myself now, but what could have been more stupid than describing all that aloud to her? That was the cause of my proud silence, that's why we sat in silence. For what could she have understood? Sixteen years old, the earliest youth – yes, what could she have understood of my justification, of my sufferings? Undeviating straightness, ignorance of life, the cheap convictions of youth, the hen-like blindness of those 'noble hearts,' and what stood for most was – the pawnbroker's shop and – enough! (And was I a villain in the pawnbroker's shop? Did not she see how I acted? Did I extort too much?)

Oh, how awful is truth on earth! That exquisite creature, that gentle spirit, that heaven – she was a tyrant, she was the insufferable tyrant and torture of my soul! I should be unfair to myself if I didn't say so! You imagine I didn't love her? Who can say that I did not love her! Do you see, it was a case of irony, the malignant irony of fate and nature! We were under a curse, the life of men in general is under a curse! (mine in particular). Of course, I understand now that I made some mistake! Something went wrong. Everything was clear, my plan was clear as daylight: 'Austere and proud, asking for no moral comfort, but suffering in silence.' And that was how it was. I was not lying, I was not lying! 'She will see for herself, later on, that it was heroic, only that she had not known how to see it, and when, some day, she divines, it she will prize me ten times more and will abase herself in the dust and fold her hands in homage' – that was my plan. But I forgot something or lost sight of it. There was something I failed to manage. But, enough, enough! And whose forgiveness am I to ask now? What is done is done. Be bolder, man, and have some pride! It is not your fault! . . .

Well, I will tell the truth, I am not afraid to face the truth; it was her fault, her fault!

CHAPTER 5

A Gentle Spirit in Revolt

Quarrels began from her suddenly beginning to pay out loans on her own account, to price things above their worth, and even, on two occasions, she deigned to enter into a dispute about it with me. I did not agree. But then the captain's widow turned up.

This old widow brought a medallion – a present from her dead husband, a souvenir, of course. I lent her thirty roubles on it. She fell to complaining, begged me to keep the thing for her – of course we do keep things. Well, in short, she came again to exchange it for a bracelet that was not worth eight roubles; I, of course, refused. She must have guessed something from my wife's eyes, anyway she came again when I was not there and my wife changed it for the medallion.

Discovering it the same day, I spoke mildly but firmly and reasonably. She was sitting on the bed, looking at the ground and tapping with her right foot on the carpet (her characteristic movement); there was an ugly smile on her lips. Then, without raising my voice in the least, I explained calmly that the money was mine, that I had a right to look at life with my own eyes and – and that when I had offered to take her into my house, I had hidden nothing from her.

She suddenly leapt up, suddenly began shaking all over and — what do you think — she suddenly stamped her foot at me; it was a wild animal, it was a frenzy, it was the frenzy of a wild animal. I was petrified with astonishment; I had never expected such an outburst. But I did not lose my head. I made no movement even, and again, in the same calm voice, I announced plainly that from that time forth I should deprive her of the part she took in my work. She laughed in my face, and walked out of the house.

The fact is, she had not the right to walk out of the house. Nowhere without me, such was the agreement before she was married. In the evening she returned; I did not utter a word.

The next day, too, she went out in the morning, and the day after again. I shut the shop and went off to her aunts. I had cut off all relations with them from the time of the wedding — I would not have them to see me, and I would not go to see them. But it turned out that she had not been with them. They listened to me with curiosity and laughed in my face: 'It serves you right,' they said. But I expected their laughter. At that point, then I bought over the younger aunt, the unmarried one, for a hundred roubles, giving her twenty-five in advance. Two days later she came to me: 'There's an officer called Efimovitch mixed up in this,' she said; 'a lieutenant who was a comrade of yours in the regiment.'

I was greatly amazed. That Efimovitch had done me more harm than anyone in the regiment, and about a month ago, being a shameless fellow, he once or twice came into the shop with a pretence of pawning something, and I remember, began laughing with my wife. I went up at the time and told him not to dare to come to me, recalling our relations; but there was no thought of anything in my head, I simply thought that he was insolent. Now the aunt suddenly informed me that she had already appointed to see him and that the whole business had been arranged by a former friend of the aunt's, the widow of a colonel, called Yulia Samsonovna. 'It's to her,' she said, 'your wife goes now.'

I will cut the story short. The business cost me three hundred roubles, but in a couple of days it had been arranged that I should stand in an adjoining room, behind closed doors, and listen to the first rendezvous between my wife and Efimovitch, tete-a-tete. Meanwhile, the evening before, a scene, brief but very memorable for me, took place between us.

She returned towards evening, sat down on the bed, looked at me sarcastically, and tapped on the carpet with her foot. Looking at her, the idea suddenly came into my mind that for the whole of the last month, or rather, the last fortnight, her character had not been her own; one might even say that it had been the opposite of her own; she had suddenly shown herself a mutinous, aggressive creature; I cannot say shameless, but regardless of decorum and eager for trouble. She went out of her way to stir up trouble. Her gentleness hindered her, though. When a girl like that rebels, however outrageously she may behave, one can always see that she is forcing herself to do it, that she is driving herself to do it, and that it is impossible for her to master and overcome her own modesty and shamefacedness. That is why such people go such lengths at times, so that one can hardly believe one's eyes. One who is accustomed to depravity, on the contrary, always softens things, acts more disgustingly, but with a show of decorum and seemliness by which she claims to be superior to you.

'Is it true that you were turned out of the regiment because you were afraid to fight a duel?' she asked suddenly, apropos of nothing – and her eyes flashed.

'It is true that by the sentence of the officers I was asked to give up my commission, though, as a fact, I had sent in my papers before that.'

'You were turned out as a coward?'

'Yes, they sentenced me as a coward. But I refused to fight a duel, not from cowardice, but because I would not submit to their tyrannical decision and send a challenge when I did not consider myself insulted. You know,' I could not refrain from adding, 'that to resist such tyranny and to accept the consequences meant showing far more manliness than fighting any kind of duel.'

I could not resist it. I dropped the phrase, as it were, in self-defence, and that was all she wanted, this fresh humiliation for me.

She laughed maliciously.

'And is it true that for three years afterwards you wandered about the streets of Petersburg like a tramp, begging for coppers and spending your nights in billiard-rooms?'

'I even spent the night in Vyazemsky's House in the Haymarket. Yes, it is true; there was much disgrace and degradation in my life after I left the regiment, but not moral degradation, because even at the time I hated what I did more than anyone. It was only the degradation of my will and my mind, and it was only caused by the desperateness of my position. But that is over . . .'

'Oh, now you are a personage – a financier!'

A hint at the pawnbroker's shop. But by then I had succeeded in recovering my mastery of myself. I saw that she was thirsting for explanations that be humiliating to me and – I did not give them. A customer rang the bell very opportunely, and I went out into the shop. An hour later, when she was dressed to go out, she stood still, facing me, and said—

'You didn't tell me anything about that, though, before our marriage?'

I made no answer and she went away.

And so next day I was standing in that room, the other side of the door, listening to hear how my fate was being decided, and in my pocket I had a revolver. She was dressed better than usual and sitting at the table, and Efimovitch was showing off before her. And after all, it turned out exactly (I say it to my credit) as I had foreseen and had assumed it would, though I was not conscious of having foreseen and assumed it. I do not know whether I express myself intelligibly.

This is what happened.

I listened for a whole hour. For a whole hour I was present at a duel between a noble, lofty woman and a worldly, corrupt, dense man with a crawling soul. And how, I wondered in amazement, how could that naive, gentle, silent girl have come to know all that?

The wittiest author of a society comedy could not have created such a scene of mockery, of naive laughter, and of the holy contempt of virtue for vice. And how brilliant her sayings, her little phrases were: what wit there was in her rapid answers, what truths in her condemnation. And, at the same time, what almost girlish simplicity. She laughed in his face at his declarations of love, at his gestures, at his proposals. Coming coarsely to the point at once, and not expecting to meet with opposition, he was utterly nonplussed. At first I might have imagined that it was simply coquetry on her part – 'the coquetry of a witty, though depraved creature to enhance her own value.' But no, the truth shone out like the sun, and to doubt was impossible. It was only an exaggerated and impulsive hatred for me that had led her, in her inexperience, to arrange this interview, but, when it came off – her eyes were opened at once. She was simply in desperate haste to mortify me, come what might, but though she had brought herself to do something so low she could not endure unseemliness. And could she, so pure and sinless, with an ideal in her heart, have been seduced by Efimovitch or any worthless snob? On the contrary, she was only moved to laughter by him. All her goodness rose up from her soul and her indignation roused her to sarcasm. I repeat, the buffoon was completely nonplussed at last and sat frowning, scarcely answering, so much so that I began to be afraid that he might insult her, from a mean desire for revenge. And I repeat again: to my credit, I listened to that scene almost without surprise. I met, as it were, nothing but what I knew well. I had gone, as it were, on purpose to meet it, believing not a word of it, not a word said against her, though I did take the revolver in my pocket – that is the truth. And could I have imagined her different? For what did I love her, for what did I prize her, for what had I married her? Oh, of course, I was quite convinced of her hate for me, but at the same time I was quite convinced of her sinlessness. I suddenly cut short the scene by opening the door. Efimovitch leapt up. I took her by the hand and suggested she should go home with me. Efimovitch recovered himself and suddenly burst into loud peals of laughter.

'Oh, to sacred conjugal rights I offer no opposition; take her away, take her away! And you know,' he shouted after me, 'though no decent man could fight you, yet from respect to your lady I am at your service . . . If you are ready to risk yourself.'

'Do you hear?' I said, stopping her for a second in the doorway.

After which not a word was said all the way home. I led her by the arm and she did not resist. On the contrary, she was greatly impressed, and this lasted after she got home. On reaching home she sat down in a chair and fixed her eyes upon me. She was extremely pale; though her lips were compressed ironically yet she looked at me with solemn and austere defiance and seemed convinced in earnest, for the minute, that I should kill her with the revolver. But I took the revolver from my pocket without a word and laid it on the table! She looked at me and at the revolver (note that the revolver was already an object familiar to her. I had kept one loaded ever since I opened the shop. I made up my mind when I set up the shop that I would not keep a huge dog or a strong manservant, as Mozer does, for instance. My cook opens the doors to my visitors. But in our trade it is impossible to be without means of self-defence in case of emergency, and I kept a loaded revolver. In early days, when first she was living in my house, she took great interest in that revolver, and asked questions about it, and I even explained its construction and working; I even persuaded her once to fire at a target. Note all that). Taking no notice of her frightened eyes, I lay down on the bed, half-undressed. I felt very much exhausted; it was by then about eleven o'clock. She went on sitting in the same place, not stirring, for another hour. Then she put out the candle and she, too, without undressing, lay down on the sofa near the wall. For the first time she did not sleep with me – note that too . . .

CHAPTER 6

A Terrible Reminiscence

Now for a terrible reminiscence . . .

I woke up, I believe, before eight o'clock, and it was very nearly broad daylight. I woke up completely to full consciousness and opened my eyes. She was standing at the table holding the revolver in her hand. She did not see that I had woken up and was looking at her. And suddenly I saw that she had begun moving towards me with the revolver in her hand. I quickly closed my eyes and pretended to be still asleep.

She came up to the bed and stood over me. I heard everything; though a dead silence had fallen I heard that silence. All at once there was a convulsive movement and, irresistibly, against my will, I suddenly opened my eyes. She was looking straight at me, straight into my eyes, and the revolver was at my temple. Our eyes met. But we looked at each other for no more than a moment. With an effort I shut my eyes again, and at the same instant I resolved that I would not stir and would not open my eyes, whatever might be awaiting me.

It does sometimes happen that people who are sound asleep suddenly open their eyes, even raise their heads for a second and look about the room, then, a moment later, they lay their heads again on the pillow unconscious, and fall asleep without understanding anything. When meeting her eyes and feeling the revolver on my forehead, I closed my eyes and remained motionless, as though in a deep sleep – she certainly might have supposed that I really was asleep, and that I had seen nothing, especially as it was utterly improbable that, after seeing what I had seen, I should shut my eyes again at such a moment.

Yes, it was improbable. But she might guess the truth all the same – that thought flashed upon my mind at once, all at the same instant. Oh, what a whirl of thoughts and sensations rushed into my mind in less than a minute. Hurrah for the electric speed of thought! In that case (so I felt), if she guessed the truth and knew that I was awake, I should crush her by my readiness to accept death, and her hand might tremble. Her determination might be shaken by a new, overwhelming impression. They say that people standing on a height have an impulse to throw themselves down. I imagine that many suicides and murders have been committed simply because the revolver has been in the hand. It is like a precipice, with an incline of an angle of forty-five degrees, down which you cannot help sliding, and something impels you irresistibly to pull the trigger. But the knowledge that I had seen, that I knew it all, and was waiting for death at her hands without a word – might hold her back on the incline.

The stillness was prolonged, and all at once I felt on my temple, on my hair, the cold contact of iron. You will ask: did I confidently expect to escape? I will answer you as God is my judge: I had no hope of it, except one chance in a hundred. Why did I accept death? But I will ask, what use was life to me after that revolver had been raised against me by the being I adored? Besides, I knew with the whole strength of my being that there was a struggle going on between us, a fearful duel for life and death, the duel fought be the coward of yesterday, rejected by his comrades for cowardice. I knew that and she knew it, if only she guessed the truth that I was not asleep.

Perhaps that was not so, perhaps I did not think that then, but yet it must have been so, even without conscious thought, because I've done nothing but think of it every hour of my life since.

But you will ask me again: why did you not save her from such wickedness? Oh! I've asked myself that question a thousand times since – every time that, with a shiver down my back, I recall that second. But at that moment my soul was plunged in dark despair! I was lost, I myself was lost – how could I save anyone? And how do you know whether I wanted to save anyone then? How can one tell what I could be feeling then?

My mind was in a ferment, though; the seconds passed; she still stood over me – and suddenly I shuddered with hope! I quickly opened my eyes. She was no longer in the room: I got out of bed: I had conquered – and she was conquered for ever!

I went to the samovar. We always had the samovar brought into the outer room and she always poured out the tea. I sat down at the table without a word and took a glass of tea from her. Five minutes later I looked at her. She was fearfully pale, even paler than the day before, and she looked at me. And suddenly . . . and suddenly, seeing that I was looking at her, she gave a pale smile with her pale lips, with a timid question in her eyes. 'So she still doubts and is asking herself: does he know or doesn't he know; did he see or didn't he?' I turned my eyes away indifferently. After tea I closed the shop, went to the market and bought an iron bedstead and a screen. Returning home, I directed that the bed should be put in the front room and shut off with a screen. It was a bed for her, but I did not say a word to her. She understood without words, through that bedstead, that I 'had seen and knew all,' and that all doubt was over. At night I left the revolver on the table, as I always did. At night she got into her new bed without a word: our marriage bond was broken, 'she was conquered but not forgiven.' At night she began to be delirious, and in the morning she had brain-fever. She was in bed for six weeks.

PART TWO

CHAPTER I

The Dream of Pride

Lukerya has just announced that she can't go on living here and that she is going away as soon as her lady is buried. I knelt down and prayed for five minutes. I wanted to pray for an hour, but I keep thinking and thinking, and always sick thoughts, and my head aches – what is the use of praying? – it's only a sin! It is strange, too, that I am not sleepy: in great, too great sorrow, after the first outbursts one is always sleepy. Men condemned to death, they say, sleep very soundly on the last night. And so it must be, it is the law of nature, otherwise their strength would not hold out . . . I lay down on the sofa but I did not sleep . . .

. . . For the six weeks of her illness we were looking after her day and night – Lukerya and I together with a trained nurse whom I had engaged from the hospital. I spared no expense – in fact, I was eager to spend my money for her. I called in Dr Shreder and paid him ten roubles a visit. When she began to get better I did not show myself so much. But why am I describing it? When she got up again, she sat quietly and silently in my room at a special table, which I had bought for her, too, about that time . . . Yes, that's the truth, we were absolutely silent; that is, we began talking afterwards, but only of the daily routine. I purposely avoided expressing myself, but I noticed that she, too, was glad not to have to say a word more than was necessary. It seemed to me that this was perfectly normal on her part: 'She is too much shattered, too completely conquered,' I thought, 'and I must let her forget and grow used to it.' In this way we were silent, but every minute I was preparing myself for the future. I thought that she was too, and it was fearfully interesting to me to guess what she was thinking about to herself then.

> I will say more: oh! of course, no one knows what I went through, moaning over her in her illness. But I stifled my moans in my own heart, even from Lukerya. I could not imagine, could not even conceive of her dying without knowing the whole truth. When she was out of danger and began to regain her health, I very quickly and completely, I remember, recovered my tranquillity. What is more, I made up my mind to defer our future as long as possible, and meanwhile to leave things just as they were. Yes, something strange and peculiar happened to me then, I cannot call it anything else: I had triumphed, and the mere consciousness of that was enough for me. So the whole winter passes. Oh! I was satisfied as I had never been before, and it lasted the whole winter.

You see, there had been a terrible external circumstance in my life which, up till then — that is, up to the catastrophe with my wife — had weighed upon me every day and every hour. I mean the loss of my reputation and my leaving the regiment. In two words, I was treated with tyrannical injustice. It is true my comrades did not love me because of my difficult character, and perhaps because of my absurd character, though it often happens that what is exalted, precious and of value to one, for some reason amuses the herd of one's companions. Oh, I was never liked, not even at school! I was always and everywhere disliked. Even Lukerya cannot like me. What happened in the regiment, though it was the result of their dislike to me, was in a sense accidental. I mention this because nothing is more mortifying and insufferable than to be ruined by an accident, which might have happened or not have happened, from an unfortunate accumulation of circumstances which might have passed over like a cloud. For an intelligent being it is humiliating. This is what happened.

In an interval, at a theatre, I went out to the refreshment bar. A hussar called A— came in and began, before all the officers present and the public, loudly talking to two other hussars, telling them that Captain Bezumtsev, of our regiment, was making a disgraceful scene in the passage and was, 'he believed, drunk.' The conversation did not go further and, indeed, it was a mistake, for Captain Bezumtsev was not drunk and the 'disgraceful scene' was not really disgraceful. The hussars began talking of something else, and the matter ended there, but the next day the story reached our regiment, and then they began saying at once that I was the only officer of our regiment in the refreshment bar at the time, and that when A— the hussar, had spoken insolently of Captain Bezumtsev, I had not gone up to A— and stopped him by remonstrating. But on what grounds could I have done so? If he had a grudge against Bezumtsev, it was their personal affair and why should I interfere? Meanwhile, the officers began to declare that it was not a personal affair, but that it concerned the regiment, and as I was the only officer of the regiment present I had thereby shown all the officers and other people in the refreshment bar that there could be officers in our regiment who were not oversensitive on the score of their own honour and the honour of their regiment. I could not agree with this view. They let me know that I could set everything right if I were willing, even now, late as it was, to demand a formal explanation from A—. I was not willing to do this, and as I was irritated I refused with pride. And thereupon I forthwith resigned my commission — that is the whole story. I left the regiment, proud but crushed in spirit. I was depressed in will and mind. Just then it was that my sister's husband in Moscow squandered all our little property and my portion of it, which was tiny enough, but the loss of it left me homeless, without a farthing. I might have taken a job in a private business, but I did not. After wearing a distinguished uniform I could not take work in a railway office. And so — if it must be shame, let it be shame; if it must be disgrace, let it be disgrace; if it must be degradation, let it be degradation — (the worse it is, the better) that was my choice. Then followed three years of gloomy memories, and even Vyazemsky's House. A year and a half ago my godmother, a wealthy old lady, died in Moscow, and to my surprise left me three thousand in her will. I thought a little and immediately decided on my course of action. I determined on setting up as a pawnbroker, without apologising to any one: money, then a home, as far as possible from memories of the past, that was my plan. Nevertheless, the gloomy past and my ruined reputation fretted me every day, every hour. But then I married. Whether it was by chance or not I don't know. But when I brought her into my home I thought I was bringing a friend, and I needed a friend so much. But I saw clearly that the friend must be trained, schooled, even conquered. Could I have explained myself straight off to a girl of sixteen with her prejudices? How, for instance, could I, without the chance help of the horrible incident with the revolver, have made her believe I was not a coward, and that I had been unjustly accused of cowardice in the regiment? But that terrible incident came just in the nick of time. Standing the test of the revolver, I scored off all my gloomy past. And though no one knew about it, she knew, and for me that was everything, because she was everything for me, all the hope of the future that I cherished in my dreams! She was the one person I had prepared for myself, and I needed no one else – and here she knew everything; she knew, at any rate, that she had been in haste to join my enemies against me unjustly. That thought enchanted me. In her eyes I could not be a scoundrel now, but at most a strange person, and that thought after all that had happened was by no means displeasing to me; strangeness is not a vice – on the contrary, it sometimes attracts the feminine heart. In fact, I purposely deferred the climax: what had happened was meanwhile, enough for my peace of mind and provided a great number of pictures and materials for my dreams. That is what is wrong, that I am a dreamer: I had enough material for my dreams, and about her, I thought she could wait.

So the whole winter passed in a sort of expectation. I liked looking at her on the sly, when she was sitting at her little table. She was busy at her needlework, and sometimes in the evening she read books taken from my bookcase. The choice of books in the bookcase must have had an influence in my favour too. She hardly ever went out. Just before dusk, after dinner, I used to take her out every day for a walk. We took a constitutional, but we were not absolutely silent, as we used to be. I tried, in fact, to make a show of our not being silent, but talking harmoniously, but as I have said already, we both avoided letting ourselves go. I did it purposely, I thought it was essential to 'give her time.' Of course, it was strange that almost till the end of the winter it did not once strike me that, though I love to watch her stealthily, I had never once, all the winter, caught her glancing at me! I thought it was timidity in her. Besides, she had an air of such timid gentleness, such weakness after her illness. Yes, better to wait and – 'she will come to you all at once of herself . . .'

That thought fascinated me beyond all words. I will add one thing; sometimes, as it were purposely, I worked myself up and brought my mind and spirit to the point of believing she had injured me. And so it went on for some time. But my anger could never be very real or violent. And I felt myself as though it were only acting. And though I had broken off our marriage by buying that bedstead and screen, I could never, never look upon her as a criminal. And not that I took a frivolous view of her crime, but because I had the sense to forgive her completely, from the very first day, even before I bought the bedstead. In fact, it is strange on my part, for I am strict in moral questions. On the contrary, in my eyes, she was so conquered, so humiliated, so crushed, that sometimes I felt agonies of pity for her, though sometimes the thought of her humiliation was actually pleasing to me. The thought of our inequality pleased me . . .

I intentionally performed several acts of kindness that winter. I excused two debts, I gave one poor woman money without any pledge. And I said nothing to my wife about it, and I didn't do it in order that she should know; but the woman came to thank me, almost on her knees. And in that way it became public property; it seemed to me that she heard about the woman with pleasure.

But spring was coming, it was mid-April, we took out the double windows and the sun began lighting up our silent room with its bright beams. But there was, as it were, a veil before my eyes and a blindness over my mind. A fatal, terrible veil! How did it happen that the scales suddenly fell from my eyes, and I suddenly saw and understood? Was it a chance, or had the hour come, or did the ray of sunshine kindle a thought, a conjecture, in my dull mind? No, it was not a thought, not a conjecture. But a chord suddenly vibrated, a feeling that had long been dead was stirred and came to life, flooding all my darkened soul and devilish pride with light. It was as though I had suddenly leaped up from my place. And, indeed, it happened suddenly and abruptly. It happened towards evening, at five o'clock, after dinner . . .

CHAPTER 2

The Veil Suddenly Falls

Two words first. A month ago I noticed a strange melancholy in her, not simply silence, but melancholy. That, too, I noticed suddenly. She was sitting at her work, her head bent over her sewing, and she did not see that I was looking at her. And it suddenly struck me that she had grown so delicate-looking, so thin, that her face was pale, her lips were white. All this, together with her melancholy, struck me all at once. I had already heard a little dry cough, especially at night. I got up at once and went off to ask Shreder to come, saying nothing to her.

Shreder came next day. She was very much surprised and looked first at Shreder and then at me.

'But I am well,' she said, with an uncertain smile.

Shreder did not examine her very carefully (these doctors are sometimes superciliously careless), he only said to me in the other room, that it was just the result of her illness, and that it wouldn't be amiss to go for a trip to the sea in the spring, or, if that were impossible to take a cottage out of town for the summer. In fact, he said nothing except that there was weakness, or something of that sort. When Shreder had gone, she said again, looking at me very earnestly—

'I am quite well, quite well.'

But as she said this she suddenly flushed, apparently from shame. Apparently it was shame. Oh! now I understand: she was ashamed that I was still her husband, that I was looking after her still as though I were a real husband. But at the time I did not understand and put down her blush to humility (the veil!).

And so, a month later, in April, at five o'clock on a bright sunny day, I was sitting in the shop making up my accounts. Suddenly I heard her, sitting in our room, at work at her table, begin softly, softly . . . singing. This novelty made an overwhelming impression upon me, and to this day I don't understand it. Till then I had hardly ever heard her sing, unless, perhaps, in those first days, when we were still able to be playful and practise shooting at a target. Then her voice was rather strong, resonant; though not quite true it was very sweet and healthy. Now her little song was so faint – it was not that it was melancholy (it was some sort of ballad), but in her voice there was something jangled, broken, as though her voice were not equal to it, as though the song itself were sick. She sang in an undertone, and suddenly, as her voice rose, it broke – such a poor little voice, it broke so pitifully; she cleared her throat and again began softly, softly singing . . .

My emotions will be ridiculed, but no one will understand why I was so moved! No, I was still not sorry for her, it was still something quite different. At the beginning, for the first minute, at any rate, I was filled with sudden perplexity and terrible amazement – a terrible and strange, painful and almost vindictive amazement: 'She is singing, and before me; has she forgotten about me?'

Completely overwhelmed, I remained where I was, then I suddenly got up, took my hat and went out, as it were, without thinking. At least I don't know why or where I was going. Lukerya began giving me my overcoat.

'She is singing?' I said to Lukerya involuntarily. She did not understand, and looked at me still without understanding; and, indeed, I was really unintelligible.

'Is it the first time she is singing?'

'No, she sometimes does sing when you are out,' answered Lukerya.

I remember everything. I went downstairs, went out into the street and walked along at random. I walked to the corner and began looking into the distance. People were passing by, they pushed against me. I did not feel it. I called a cab and told the man, I don't know why, to drive to Politseysky Bridge. Then suddenly changed my mind and gave him twenty kopecks.

'That's for my having troubled you,' I said, with a meaningless laugh, but a sort of ecstasy was suddenly shining within me.

I returned home, quickening my steps. The poor little jangled, broken note was ringing in my heart again. My breath failed me. The veil was falling, was falling from my eyes! Since she sang before me, she had forgotten me – that is what was clear and terrible. My heart felt it. But rapture was glowing in my soul and it overcame my terror.

Oh! the irony of fate! Why, there had been nothing else, and could have been nothing else but that rapture in my soul all the winter, but where had I been myself all the winter? Had I been there together with my soul? I ran up the stairs in great haste, I don't know whether I went in timidly. I only remember that the whole floor seemed to be rocking and I felt as though I were floating on a river. I went into the room. She was sitting in the same place as before, with her head cursorily and without interest at me; it was hardly a look but just a habitual and indifferent movement upon somebody's coming into the room.

I went straight up and sat down beside her in a chair abruptly, as though I were mad. She looked at me quickly, seeming frightened; I took her hand and I don't remember what I said to her – that is, tried to say, for I could not even speak properly. My voice broke and would not obey me and I did not know what to say. I could only gasp for breath.

'Let us talk . . . you know . . . tell me something!' I muttered something stupid. Oh! how could I help being stupid? She started again and drew back in great alarm, looking at my face, but suddenly there was an expression of stern surprise in her eyes. Yes, surprise and stern. She looked at me with wide-open eyes. That sternness, that stern surprise shattered me at once: 'So you still expect love? Love?' that surprise seemed to be asking, though she said nothing. But I read it all, I read it all. Everything within me seemed quivering, and I simply fell down at her feet. Yes, I grovelled at her feet. She jumped up quickly, but I held her forcibly by both hands.

And I fully understood my despair – I understood it! But, would you believe it? ecstasy was surging up in my head so violently that I thought I should die. I kissed her feet in delirium and rapture. Yes, in immense, infinite rapture, and that, in spite of understanding all the hopelessness of my despair. I wept, said something, but could not speak. Her alarm and amazement were followed by some uneasy misgiving, some grave question, and she looked at me strangely, wildly even; she wanted to understand something quickly and she smiled. She was horribly ashamed at my kissing her feet and she drew them back. But I kissed the place on the floor where her foot had rested. She saw it and suddenly began laughing with shame (you know how it is when people laugh with shame). She became hysterical, I saw that her hands trembled – I did not think about that but went on muttering that I loved her, that I would not get up. 'Let me kiss your dress . . . and worship you like this all my life.' . . . I don't know, I don't remember – but suddenly she broke into sobs and trembled all over. A terrible fit of hysterics followed. I had frightened her.

I carried her to the bed. When the attack had passed off, sitting on the edge of the bed, with a terribly exhausted look, she took my two hands and begged me to calm myself: 'Come, come, don't distress yourself, be calm!' and she began crying again. All that evening I did not leave her side. I kept telling her I should take her to Boulogne to bathe in the sea now, at once, in a fortnight, that she had such a broken voice, I had heard it that afternoon, that I would shut up the shop, that I would sell it to Dobronravov, that everything should begin afresh and, above all, Boulogne, Boulogne! She listened and was still afraid. She grew more and more afraid. But that was not what mattered most for me: what mattered most to me was the more and more irresistible longing to fall at her feet again, and again to kiss and kiss the spot where her foot had rested, and to worship her; and – 'I ask nothing, nothing more of you,' I kept repeating, 'do not answer me, take no notice of me, only let me watch you from my corner, treat me as your dog, your thing . . .' She was crying.

'I thought you would let me go on like that,' suddenly broke from her unconsciously, so unconsciously that, perhaps, she did not notice what she had said, and yet – oh, that was the most significant, momentous phrase she uttered that evening, the easiest for me to understand, and it stabbed my heart as though with a knife! It explained everything to me, everything, but while she was beside me, before my eyes, I could not help hoping and was fearfully happy. Oh, I exhausted her fearfully that evening. I understood that, but I kept thinking that I should alter everything directly. At last, towards night, she was utterly exhausted. I persuaded her to go to sleep and she fell sound asleep at once. I expected her to be delirious, she was a little delirious, but very slightly. I kept getting up every minute in the night and going softly in my slippers to look at her. I wrung my hands over her, looking at that frail creature in that wretched little iron bedstead which I had bought for three roubles. I knelt down, but did not dare to kiss her feet in her sleep (without her consent). I began praying but leapt up again. Lukerya kept watch over me and came in and out from the kitchen. I went in to her, and told her to go to bed, and that tomorrow 'things would be quite different.'

And I believed in this, blindly, madly.

Oh, I was brimming over with rapture, rapture! I was eager for the next day. Above all, I did not believe that anything could go wrong, in spite of the symptoms. Reason had not altogether come back to me, though the veil had fallen from my eyes, and for a long, long time it did not come back – not till today, not till this very day! Yes, and how could it have come back then: why, she was still alive then; why, she was here before my eyes, and I was before her eyes: 'Tomorrow she will wake up and I will tell her all this, and she will see it all.' That was how I reasoned then, simply and clearly, because I was in an ecstasy! My great idea was the trip to Boulogne. I kept thinking for some reason that Boulogne would be everything, that there was something final and decisive about Boulogne. 'To Boulogne, to Boulogne!' . . . I waited frantically for the morning.

[illegible]

CHAPTER 3

I Understand Too Well

But you know that was only a few days ago, five days ago, last Tuesday! Yes, yes, if there had only been a little longer, if she had only waited a little – and I would have dissipated the darkness! – It was not as though she had not recovered her calmness. The very next day she listened to me with a smile, in spite of her confusion . . . All this time, all these five days, she was either confused or ashamed. She was afraid, too, very much afraid. I don't dispute it, I am not so mad as to deny it. It was terror, but how could she help being frightened? We had so long been strangers to one another, had grown so alienated from one another, and suddenly all this . . . But I did not look at her terror. I was dazzled by the new life beginning! . . . It is true, it is undoubtedly true that I made a mistake. There were even, perhaps, many mistakes. When I woke up next day, the first thing in the morning (that was on Wednesday), I made a mistake: I suddenly made her my friend. I was in too great a hurry, but a confession was necessary, inevitable – more than a confession! I did not even hide what I had hidden from myself all my life. I told her straight out that the whole winter I had been doing nothing but brood over the certainty of her love. I made clear to her that my money-lending had been simply the degradation of my will and my mind, my personal idea of self-castigation and self-exaltation. I explained to her that I really had been cowardly that time in the refreshment bar, that it was owing to my temperament, to my self-consciousness. I was impressed by the surroundings, by the theatre: I was doubtful how I should succeed and whether it would be stupid. I was not afraid of a duel, but of its being stupid . . . and afterwards I would not own it and tormented everyone and had tormented her for it, and had married her so as to torment her for it. In fact, for the most part I talked as though in delirium. She herself took my hands and made me leave off. 'You are exaggerating . . . you are distressing yourself,' and again there were tears, again almost hysterics! She kept begging me not to say all this, not to recall it.

I took no notice of her entreaties, or hardly noticed them: 'Spring, Boulogne! There there would be sunshine, there our new sunshine,' I kept saying that! I shut up the shop and transferred it to Dobronravov. I suddenly suggested to her giving all our money to the poor except the three thousand left me by my godmother, which we would spend on going to Boulogne, and then we would come back and begin a new life of real work. So we decided, for she said nothing . . . She only smiled. And I believe she smiled chiefly from delicacy, for fear of disappointing me. I saw, of course, that I was burdensome to her, don't imagine I was so stupid or egoistic as not to see it. I saw it all, all, to the smallest detail, I saw better than any one; all the hopelessness of my position stood revealed.

I told her everything about myself and about her. And about Lukerya. I told her that I had wept . . . Oh, of course, I changed the conversation. I tried, too, not to say a word more about certain things. And, indeed, she did revive once or twice – I remember it, I remember it! Why do you say I looked at her and saw nothing? And if only this had not happened, everything would have come to life again. Why, only the day before yesterday, when we were talking of reading and what she had been reading that winter, she told me something herself, and laughed as she told me, recalling the scene of Gil Blas and the Archbishop of Granada. And with that sweet, childish laughter, just as in the old days when we were eager (one instant! one instant!); how glad I was! I was awfully struck, though, by the story of the Archbishop; so she had found peace of mind and happiness enough to laugh at that literary masterpiece while she was sitting there in the winter. So then she had begun to be fully at rest, had begun to believe confidently 'that I should leave her like that. I thought you would leave me like that,' those were the words she uttered then on Tuesday! Oh! the thought of a child of ten! And you know she believed it, she believed that really everything would remain like that: she at her table and I at mine, and we both should go on like that till we were sixty. And all at once – I come forward, her husband, and the husband wants love! Oh, the delusion! Oh, my blindness!

It was a mistake, too, that I looked at her with rapture; I ought to have controlled myself, as it was my rapture frightened her. But, indeed, I did control myself, I did not kiss her feet again. I never made a sign of . . . well, that I was her husband – oh, there was no thought of that in my mind, I only worshipped her! But, you know, I couldn't be quite silent, I could not refrain from speaking altogether! I suddenly said to her frankly, that I enjoyed her conversation and that I thought her incomparably more cultured and developed than I. She flushed crimson and said in confusion that I exaggerated. Then, like a fool, I could not resist telling her how delighted I had been when I had stood behind the door listening to her duel, the duel of innocence with that low cad, and how I had enjoyed her cleverness, the brilliance of her wit, and, at the same time, her childlike simplicity. She seemed to shudder all over, was murmuring again that I exaggerated, but suddenly her whole face darkened, she hid it in her hands and broke into sobs . . . Then I could not restrain myself: again I fell at her feet, again I began kissing her feet, and again it ended in a fit of hysterics, just as on Tuesday. That was yesterday evening – and – in the morning . . .

In the morning! Madman! why, that morning was today, just now, only just now!

Listen and try to understand: why, when we met by the samovar (it was after yesterday's hysterics), I was actually struck by her calmness, that is the actual fact! And all night I had been trembling with terror over what happened yesterday. But suddenly she came up to me and, clasping her hands (this morning, this morning!) began telling me that she was a criminal, that she knew it, that her crime had been torturing her all the winter, was torturing her now . . . That she appreciated my generosity . . . 'I will be your faithful wife, I will respect you . . .'

Then I leapt up and embraced her like a madman. I kissed her, kissed her face, kissed her lips like a husband for the first time after a long separation. And why did I go out this morning, only two hours . . . our passports for abroad . . . Oh, God! if only I had come back five minutes, only five minutes earlier! . . . That crowd at our gates, those eyes all fixed upon me. Oh, God!

Lukerya says (oh! I will not let Lukerya go now for anything. She knows all about it, she has been here all the winter, she will tell me everything!), she says that when I had gone out of the house and only about twenty minutes before I came back — she suddenly went into our room to her mistress to ask her something, I don't remember what, and saw that her ikon (that same ikon of the Mother of God) had been taken down and was standing before her on the table, and her mistress seemed to have only just been praying before it. 'What are you doing, mistress?' 'Nothing, Lukerya, run along.' 'Wait a minute, Lukerya.' 'She came up and kissed me.' 'Are you happy, mistress?' I said. 'Yes, Lukerya,' and she smiled, but so strangely. So strangely that Lukerya went back ten minutes later to have a look at her.

'She was standing by the wall, close to the window, she had laid her arm against the wall, and her head was pressed on her arm, she was standing like that thinking. And she was standing so deep in thought that she did not hear me come and look at her from the other room. She seemed to be smiling — standing, thinking and smiling.

I looked at her, turned softly and went out wondering to myself, and suddenly I heard the window opened. I went in at once to say: "It's fresh, mistress; mind you don't catch cold," and suddenly I saw she had got on the window and was standing there, her full height, in the open window, with her back to me, holding the ikon in her hand. My heart sank on the spot. I cried, "Mistress, mistress." She heard, made a movement to turn back to me, but, instead of turning back, took a step forward, pressed the ikon to her bosom, and flung herself out of the window.'

I only remember that when I went in at the gate she was still warm. The worst of it was they were all looking at me. At first they shouted and then suddenly they were silent, and then all of them moved away from me . . . and she was lying there with the ikon. I remember, as it were, in a darkness, that I went up to her in silence and looked at her a long while. But all came round me and said something to me. Lukerya was there too, but I did not see her. She says she said something to me. I only remember that workman. He kept shouting to me that, 'Only a handful of blood came from her mouth, a handful, a handful!' and he pointed to the blood on a stone. I believe I touched the blood with my finger, I smeared my finger, I looked at my finger (that I remember), and he kept repeating: 'a handful, a handful!'

'What do you mean by a handful?' I yelled with all my might, I am told, and I lifted up my hands and rushed at him.

Oh, wild! wild! Delusion! Monstrous! Impossible!

CHAPTER 4

I Was Only Five Minutes Too Late

Is it not so? Is it likely? Can one really say it was possible? What for, why did this woman die?

Oh, believe me, I understand, but why she dies is still a question. She was frightened of my love, asked herself seriously whether to accept it or not, could not bear the question and preferred to die. I know, I know, no need to rack my brains: she had made too many promises, she was afraid she could not keep them – it is clear. There are circumstances about it quite awful.

For why did she die? That is still a question, after all. The question hammers, hammers at my brain. I would have left her like that if she had wanted to remain like that. She did not believe it, that's what it was! No – no. I am talking nonsense, it was not that at all. It was simply because with me she had to be honest – if she loved me, she would have had to love me altogether, and not as she would have loved the grocer. And as she was too chaste, too pure, to consent to such love as the grocer wanted she did not want to deceive me. Did not want to deceive me with half love, counterfeiting love, or a quarter love. They are honest, too honest, that is what it is! I wanted to instil breadth of heart in her, in those days, do you remember? A strange idea.

It is awfully interesting to know: did she respect me or not? I don't know whether she despised me or not. I don't believe she did despise me. It is awfully strange: why did it never once enter my head all the winter that she despised me? I was absolutely convinced of the contrary up to that moment when she looked at me with stern surprise. Stern it was. I understood once for all, for ever! Ah, let her, let her despise me all her life even, only let her be living! Only yesterday she was walking about, talking. I simply can't understand how she threw herself out of the window! And how could I have imagined it five minutes before? I have called Lukerya. I won't let Lukerya go now for anything!

Oh, we might still have understood each other! We had simply become terribly estranged from one another during the winter, but couldn't we have grown used to each other again? Why, why, couldn't we have come together again and begun a new life again? I am generous, she was too — that was a point in common! Only a few more words, another two days — no more, and she would have understood everything.

What is most mortifying of all is that it is chance — simply a barbarous, lagging chance. That is what is mortifying! Five minutes, only five minutes too late! Had I come five minutes earlier, the moment would have passed away like a cloud, and it would never have entered her head again. And it would have ended by her understanding it all. But now again empty rooms, and me alone. Here the pendulum is ticking; it does not care, it has no pity . . . There is no one – that's the misery of it!

I keep walking about, I keep walking about. I know, I know, you need not tell me; it amuses you, you think it absurd that I complain of chance and those five minutes. But it is evident. Consider one thing: she did not even leave a note, to say, 'Blame no one for my death,' as people always do. Might she not have thought that Lukerya might get into trouble. 'She was alone with her,' might have been said, 'and pushed her out.' In any case she would have been taken up by the police if it had not happened that four people, from the windows, from the lodge, and from the yard, had seen her stand with the ikon in her hands and jump out of it herself. But that, too, was a chance, that the people were standing there and saw her. No, it was all a moment, only an irresponsible moment. A sudden impulse, a fantasy! What if she did pray before the ikon? It does not follow that she was facing death. The whole impulse lasted, perhaps, only some ten minutes; it was all decided, perhaps, while she stood against the wall with her head on her arm, smiling. The idea darted into her brain, she turned giddy and – and could not resist it.

Say what you will, it was clearly misunderstanding. It could have been possible to live with me. And what if it were anaemia? Was it simply from poorness of blood, from the flagging of vital energy? She had grown tired during the winter, that was what it was . . .

I was too late!!!

How thin she is in her coffin, how sharp her nose has

grown! Her eyelashes lie straight as arrows. And, you know, when she fell, nothing was crushed, nothing was broken! Nothing but that 'handful of blood.' A dessert-spoonful, that is. From internal injury. A strange thought: if only it were possible not to bury her? For if they take her away, then . . . oh, no, it is almost incredible that they take her away! I am not mad and I am not raving – on the contrary, my mind was never so lucid – but what shall I do when again there is no one, only the two rooms, and me alone with the pledges? Madness, madness, madness! I worried her to death, that is what it is!

What are your laws to me now? What do I care for your customs, your morals, your life, your state, your faith! Let your judge judge me, let me be brought before your court, let me be tried by jury, and I shall say that I admit nothing. The judge will shout, 'Be silent, officer.' And I will shout to him, 'What power have you now that I will obey? Why did blind, inert force destroy that which was dearest of all? What are your laws to me now? They are nothing to me.' Oh, I don't care!

She was blind, blind! She is dead, she does not hear! You do not know with what paradise I would have surrounded you. There was paradise in my soul, I would have made it blossom around you! Well, you wouldn't have loved me – so be it, what of it? Things should still have been like that, everything should have remained like that. You should only have talked to me as a friend – we could have rejoiced and laughed with joy looking at one another. And so we should have lived. And if you had loved another – well, so be it, so be it! You should have walked with him laughing, and I should have watched you from the other side of the street . . . Oh, anything, anything, if only she would open her eyes just once! For one instant, only one! If she would look at me as she did this morning, when she stood before me and made a vow to be a faithful wife! Oh, in one look she would have understood it all!

Oh, blind force! Oh, nature! Men are alone on earth – that is what is dreadful! 'Is there a living man in the country?' cried the Russian hero. I cry the same, though I am not a hero, and no one answers my cry. They say the sun gives life to the universe. The sun is rising and – look at it, is it not dead? Everything is dead and everywhere there are dead. Men are alone – around them is silence – that is the earth! 'Men, love one another' – who said that? Whose commandment is that? The pendulum ticks callously, heartlessly. Two o'clock at night. Her little shoes are standing by the little bed, as though waiting for her . . . No, seriously, when they take her away tomorrow, what will become of me?

A Faint Heart

Under the same roof in the same flat on the same fourth storey lived two young men, colleagues in the service, Arkady Ivanovitch Nefedevitch and Vasya Shumkov . . . The author of course, feels the necessity of explaining to the reader why one is given his full title, while the other's name is abbreviated, if only that such a mode of expression may not be regarded as unseemly and rather familiar. But, to do so, it would first be necessary to explain and describe the rank and years and calling and duty in the service, and even, indeed, the characters of the persons concerned; and since there are so many writers who begin in that way, the author of the proposed story, solely in order to be unlike them (that is, some people will perhaps say, entirely on account of his boundless vanity), decides to begin straightaway with action. Having completed this introduction, he begins.

Towards six o'clock on New Year's Eve Shumkov returned home. Arkady Ivanovitch, who was lying on the bed, woke up and looked at his friend with half-closed eyes. He saw that Vasya had on his very best trousers and a very clean shirt front. That, of course, struck him.

'Where had Vasya to go like that? And he had not dined at home either!' Meanwhile, Shumkov had lighted a candle, and Arkady Ivanovitch guessed immediately that his friend was intending to wake him accidentally. Vasya did, in fact, clear his throat twice, walked twice up and down the room, and at last, quite accidentally, let the pipe, which he had begun filling in the corner by the stove, slip out of his hands. Arkady Ivanovitch laughed to himself.

'Vasya, give over pretending!' he said.

'Arkasha, you are not asleep?'

'I really cannot say for certain; it seems to me I am not.'

'Oh, Arkasha! How are you, dear boy? Well, brother! Well, brother! . . . You don't know what I have to tell you!'

'I certainly don't know; come here.'

As though expecting this, Vasya went up to him at once, not at all anticipating, however, treachery from Arkady Ivanovitch. The other seized him very adroitly by the arms, turned him over, held him down, and began, as it is called, 'strangling' his victim, and apparently this proceeding afforded the lighthearted Arkady Ivanovitch great satisfaction.

'Caught!' he cried. 'Caught!'

'Arkasha, Arkasha, what are you about? Let me go. For goodness' sake, let me go, I shall crumple my dress coat!'

'As though that mattered! What do you want with a dress coat? Why were you so confiding as to put yourself in my hands? Tell me, where have you been? Where have you dined?'

'Arkasha, for goodness' sake, let me go!'

'Where have you dined?'

'Why, it's about that I want to tell you.'

'Tell away, then.'

'But first let me go.'

'Not a bit of it, I won't let you go till you tell me!'

'Arkasha! Arkasha! But do you understand, I can't – it is utterly impossible!' cried Vasya, helplessly wriggling out of his friend's powerful clutches, 'you know there are subjects!'

'How – subjects?' . . .

'Why, subjects that you can't talk about in such a position without losing your dignity; it's utterly impossible; it would make it ridiculous, and this is not a ridiculous matter, it is important.'

'Here, he's going in for being important! That's a new idea! You tell me so as to make me laugh, that's how you must tell me; I don't want anything important; or else you are no true friend of mine. Do you call yourself a friend? Eh?'

'Arkasha, I really can't!'

'Well, I don't want to hear . . .'

'Well, Arkasha!' began Vasya, lying across the bed and doing his utmost to put all the dignity possible into his words. 'Arkasha! If you like, I will tell you; only . . .'

'Well, what? . . .'

'Well, I am engaged to be married!'

Without uttering another word Arkady Ivanovitch took Vasya up in his arms like a baby, though the latter was by no means short, but rather long and thin, and began dexterously carrying him up and down the room, pretending that he was hushing him to sleep.

'I'll put you in your swaddling clothes, Master Bridegroom,' he kept saying. But seeing that Vasya lay in his arms, not stirring or uttering a word, he thought better of it at once, and reflecting that the joke had gone too far, set him down in the middle of the room and kissed him on the cheek in the most genuine and friendly way.

'Vasya, you are not angry?'

'Arkasha, listen . . .'

'Come, it's New Year's Eve.'

'Oh, I'm all right; but why are you such a madman, such a scatterbrain? How many times I have told you: Arkasha, it's really not funny, not funny at all!'

'Oh, well, you are not angry?'

'Oh, I'm all right; am I ever angry with anyone! But you have wounded me, do you understand?'

'But how have I wounded you? In what way?'

'I come to you as to a friend, with a full heart, to pour out my soul to you, to tell you of my happiness . . .'

'What happiness? Why don't you speak? . . .'

'Oh, well, I am going to get married!' Vasya answered with vexation, for he really was a little exasperated.

'You! You are going to get married! So you really mean it?' Arkasha cried at the top of his voice. 'No, no . . . but what's this? He talks like this and his tears are flowing . . . Vasya, my little Vasya, don't, my little son! Is it true, really?' And Arkady Ivanovitch flew to hug him again.

'Well, do you see, how it is now?' said Vasya. 'You are kind, of course, you are a friend, I know that. I come to you with such joy, such rapture, and all of a sudden I have to disclose all the joy of my heart, all my rapture struggling across the bed, in an undignified way . . . You understand, Arkasha,' Vasya went on, half laughing. 'You see, it made it seem comic: and in a sense I did not belong to myself at that minute. I could not let this be slighted . . . What's more, if you had asked me her name, I swear, I would sooner you killed me than have answered you.'

'But, Vasya, why did you not speak! You should have told me all about it sooner and I would not have played the fool!' cried Arkady Ivanovitch in genuine despair.

'Come, that's enough, that's enough! Of course, that's how it is . . . You know what it all comes from – from my having a good heart. What vexes me is, that I could not tell you as I wanted to, making you glad and happy, telling you nicely and initiating you into my secret properly . . . Really, Arkasha, I love you so much that I believe if it were not for you I shouldn't be getting married, and, in fact, I shouldn't be living in this world at all!'

Arkady Ivanovitch, who was excessively sentimental, cried and laughed at once as he listened to Vasya. Vasya did the same. Both flew to embrace one another again and forgot the past.

'How is it – how is it? Tell me all about it, Vasya! I am astonished, excuse me, brother, but I am utterly astonished; it's a perfect thunderbolt, by Jove! Nonsense, nonsense, brother, you have made it up, you've really made it up, you are telling fibs!' cried Arkady Ivanovitch, and he actually looked into Vasya's face with genuine uncertainty, but seeing in it the radiant confirmation of a positive intention of being married as soon as possible, threw himself on the bed and began rolling from side to side in ecstasy till the walls shook.

'Vasya, sit here,' he said at last, sitting down on the bed.

'I really don't know, brother, where to begin!'

They looked at one another in joyful excitement.

'Who is she, Vasya?'

'The Artemyevs! . . .' Vasya pronounced, in a voice weak with emotion.

'No?'

'Well, I did buzz into your ears about them at first, and then I shut up, and you noticed nothing. Ah, Arkasha, if you knew how hard it was to keep it from you; but I was afraid, afraid to speak! I thought it would all go wrong, and you know I was in love, Arkasha! My God! my God! You see this was the trouble,' he began, pausing continually from agitation, 'she had a suitor a year ago, but he was suddenly ordered somewhere; I knew him – he was a fellow, bless him! Well, he did not write at all, he simply vanished. They waited and waited, wondering what it meant . . . Four months ago he suddenly came back married, and has never set foot within their doors! It was coarse – shabby! And they had no one to stand up for them. She cried and cried, poor girl, and I fell in love with her . . . indeed, I had been in love with her long before, all the time! I began comforting her, and was always going there . . . Well, and I really don't know how it has all come about, only she came to love me; a week ago I could not restrain myself, I cried, I sobbed, and told her everything – well, that I love her – everything, in fact! . . . "I am ready to love you, too, Vassily Petrovitch, only I am a poor girl, don't make a mock of me; I don't dare to love any one." Well, brother, you understand! You understand? . . . On that we got engaged on the spot. I kept thinking and thinking and thinking and thinking, I said to her, "How are we to tell your mother?" She said, "It will be hard, wait a little; she's afraid, and now maybe she would not let you have me; she keeps crying, too." Without telling her I blurted it out to her mother today. Lizanka fell on her knees before her, I did the same . . . well, she gave us her blessing. Arkasha, Arkasha! My dear fellow! We will live together. No, I won't part from you for anything.'

'Vasya, look at you as I may, I can't believe it. I don't believe it, I swear. I keep feeling as though . . . Listen, how can you be engaged to be married? . . . How is it I didn't know, eh? Do you know, Vasya, I will confess it to you now. I was thinking of getting married myself; but now since you are going to be married, it is just as good! Be happy, be happy! . . .'

'Brother, I feel so lighthearted now, there is such sweetness in my soul . . .' said Vasya, getting up and pacing about the room excitedly. 'Don't you feel the same? We shall be poor, of course, but we shall be happy; and you know it is not a wild fancy; our happiness is not a fairy tale; we shall be happy in reality! . . .'

'Vasya, Vasya, listen!'

'What?' said Vasya, standing before Arkady Ivanovitch.

'The idea occurs to me; I am really afraid to say it to you . . . Forgive me, and settle my doubts. What are you going to live on? You know I am delighted that you are going to be married, of course, I am delighted, and I don't know what to do with myself, but – what are you going to live on? Eh?'

'Oh, good Heavens! What a fellow you are, Arkasha!' said Vasya, looking at Nefedevitch in profound astonishment. 'What do you mean? Even her old mother, even she did not think of that for two minutes when I put it all clearly before her. You had better ask what they are living on! They have five hundred roubles a year between the three of them: the pension, which is all they have, since the father died. She and her old mother and her little brother, whose schooling is paid for out of that income too – that is how they live! It's you and I are the capitalists! Some good years it works out to as much as seven hundred for me.'

'I say, Vasya, excuse me; I really . . . you know I . . . I am only thinking how to prevent things going wrong. How do you mean, seven hundred? It's only three hundred . . .'

'Three hundred! . . . And Yulian Mastakovitch? Have you forgotten him?'

'Yulian Mastakovitch? But you know that's uncertain, brother; that's not the same thing as three hundred roubles of secure salary, where every rouble is a friend you can trust. Yulian Mastakovitch, of course, he's a great man, in fact, I respect him, I understand him, though he is so far above us; and, by Jove, I love him, because he likes you and gives you something for your work, though he might not pay you, but simply order a clerk to work for him – but you will agree, Vasya . . . Let me tell you, too, I am not talking nonsense. I admit in all Petersburg you won't find a handwriting like your handwriting, I am ready to allow that to you,' Nefedevitch concluded, not without enthusiasm. 'But, God forbid! you may displease him all at once, you may not satisfy him, your work with him may stop, he may take another clerk — all sorts of things may happen, in fact! You know, Yulian Mastakovitch may be here today and gone tomorrow . . .'

'Well, Arkasha, the ceiling might fall on our heads this minute.'

'Oh, of course, of course, I mean nothing.'

'But listen, hear what I have got to say — you know, I don't see how he can part with me . . . No, hear what I have to say! hear what I have to say! You see, I perform all my duties punctually; you know how kind he is, you know, Arkasha, he gave me fifty roubles in silver today!'

'Did he really, Vasya? A bonus for you?'

'Bonus, indeed, it was out of his own pocket. He said: "Why, you have had no money for five months, brother, take some if you want it; thank you, I am satisfied with you." . . . Yes, really! "Yes, you don't work for me for nothing," said he. He did, indeed, that's what he said. It brought tears into my eyes, Arkasha. Good Heavens, yes!'

'I say, Vasya, have you finished copying those papers? . . .'

'No . . . I haven't finished them yet.'

'Vas . . . ya! My angel! What have you been doing?'

'Listen, Arkasha, it doesn't matter, they are not wanted for another two days, I have time enough . . .'

'How is it you have not done them?'

'That's all right, that's all right. You look so horror-stricken that you turn me inside out and make my heart ache! You are always going on at me like this! He's for ever crying out: Oh, oh, oh!!! Only consider, what does it matter? Why, I shall finish it, of course I shall finish it . . .'

'What if you don't finish it?' cried Arkady, jumping up, 'and he has made you a present today! And you going to be married . . . Tut, tut, tut! . . .'

'It's all right, it's all right,' cried Shumkov, 'I shall sit down directly, I shall sit down this minute.'

'How did you come to leave it, Vasya?'

'Oh, Arkasha! How could I sit down to work! Have I been in a fit state? Why, even at the office I could scarcely sit still, I could scarcely bear the beating of my heart . . . Oh! oh! Now I shall work all night, and I shall work all tomorrow night, and the night after, too — and I shall finish it.'

'Is there a great deal left?'

'Don't hinder me, for goodness' sake, don't hinder me; hold your tongue.'

Arkady Ivanovitch went on tip-toe to the bed and sat down, then suddenly wanted to get up, but was obliged to sit down again, remembering that he might interrupt him, though he could not sit still for excitement: it was evident that the news had thoroughly upset him, and the first thrill of delight had not yet passed off. He glanced at Shumkov; the latter glanced at him, smiled, and shook his finger at him, then, frowning severely (as though all his energy and the success of his work depended upon it), fixed his eyes on the papers.

It seemed that he, too, could not yet master his emotion; he kept changing his pen, fidgeting in his chair, re-arranging things, and setting to work again, but his hand trembled and refused to move.

'Arkasha, I've talked to them about you,' he cried suddenly, as though he had just remembered it.

'Yes,' cried Arkasha, 'I was just wanting to ask you that. Well?'

'Well, I'll tell you everything afterwards. Of course, it is my own fault, but it quite went out of my head that I didn't mean to say anything till I had written four pages, but I thought of you and of them. I really can't write, brother, I keep thinking about you . . .'

Vasya smiled.

A silence followed.

'Phew! What a horrid pen,' cried Shumkov, flinging it on the table in vexation. He took another.

'Vasya! listen! one word . . .'

'Well, make haste, and for the last time.'

'Have you a great deal left to do?'

'Ah, brother!' Vasya frowned, as though there could be nothing more terrible and murderous in the whole world than such a question. 'A lot, a fearful lot.'

'Do you know, I have an idea—'

'What?'

'Oh, never mind, never mind; go on writing.'

'Why, what? what?'

'It's past six, Vasya.'

Here Nefedevitch smiled and winked slyly at Vasya, though with a certain timidity, not knowing how Vasya would take it.

'Well, what is it?' said Vasya, throwing down his pen, looking him straight in the face and actually turning pale with excitement.

'Do you know what?'

'For goodness' sake, what is it?'

'I tell you what, you are excited, you won't get much done . . . Stop, stop, stop! I have it, I have it – listen,' said Nefedevitch, jumping up from the bed in delight, preventing Vasya from speaking and doing his utmost to ward off all objections; 'first of all you must get calm, you must pull yourself together, mustn't you?'

'Arkasha, Arkasha!' cried Vasya, jumping up from his chair, 'I will work all night, I will, really.'

'Of course, of course, you won't go to bed till morning.'

'I won't go to bed, I won't go to bed at all.'

'No, that won't do, that won't do: you must sleep, go to bed at five. I will call you at eight. Tomorrow is a holiday; you can sit and scribble away all day long . . . Then the night and – but have you a great deal left to do?'

'Yes, look, look!'

Vasya, quivering with excitement and suspense, showed the manuscript: 'Look!'

'I say, brother, that's not much.'

'My dear fellow, there's some more of it,' said Vasya, looking very timidly at Nefedevitch, as though the decision whether he was to go or not depended upon the latter.

'How much?'

'Two signatures.'

'Well, what's that? Come, I tell you what. We shall have time to finish it, by Jove, we shall!'

'Arkasha!'

'Vasya, listen! Tonight, on New Year's Eve, everyone is at home with his family. You and I are the only ones without a home or relations . . . Oh, Vasya!'

Nefedevitch clutched Vasya and hugged him in his leonine arms.

'Arkasha, it's settled.'

'Vasya, boy, I only wanted to say this. You see, Vasya — listen, bandy-legs, listen! . . .'

Arkady stopped, with his mouth open, because he could not speak for delight. Vasya held him by the shoulders, gazed into his face and moved his lips, as though he wanted to speak for him.

'Well,' he brought out at last.

'Introduce me to them today.'

'Arkady, let us go to tea there. I tell you what, I tell you what. We won't even stay to see in the New Year, we'll come away earlier,' cried Vasya, with genuine inspiration.

'That is, we'll go for two hours, neither more nor less . . .'

'And then separation till I have finished . . .'

'Vasya, boy!'

'Arkady!'

Three minutes later Arkady was dressed in his best. Vasya did nothing but brush himself, because he had been in such haste to work that he had not changed his trousers.

They hurried out into the street, each more pleased

than the other. Their way lay from the Petersburg Side to Kolomna. Arkady Ivanovitch stepped out boldly and vigorously, so that from his walk alone one could see how glad he was at the good fortune of his friend, who was more and more radiant with happiness. Vasya trotted along with shorter steps, though his deportment was none the less dignified. Arkady Ivanovitch, in fact, had never seen him before to such advantage. At that moment he actually felt more respect for him, and Vasya's physical defect, of which the reader is not yet aware (Vasya was slightly deformed), which always called forth a feeling of loving sympathy in Arkady Ivanovitch's kind heart, contributed to the deep tenderness the latter felt for him at this moment, a tenderness of which Vasya was in every way worthy. Arkady Ivanovitch felt ready to weep with happiness, but he restrained himself.

'Where are you going, where are you going, Vasya? It is nearer this way,' he cried, seeing that Vasya was making in the direction of Voznesenky.

'Hold your tongue, Arkasha.'

'It really is nearer, Vasya.'

'Do you know what, Arkasha?' Vasya began mysteriously, in a voice quivering with joy, 'I tell you what, I want to take Lizanka a little present.'

'What sort of present?'

'At the corner here, brother, is Madame Leroux's, a wonderful shop.'

'Well.'

'A cap, my dear, a cap; I saw such a charming little cap today. I inquired, I was told it was the *façon Manon*

Lescaut – a delightful thing. Cherry-coloured ribbons, and if it is not dear . . . Arkasha, even if it is dear . . .'

'I think you are superior to any of the poets, Vasya. Come along.'

They ran along, and two minutes later went into the shop. They were met by a black-eyed Frenchwoman with curls, who, from the first glance at her customers, became as joyous and happy as they, even happier, if one may say so. Vasya was ready to kiss Madame Leroux in his delight . . .

'Arkasha,' he said in an undertone, casting a casual glance at all the grand and beautiful things on little wooden stands on the huge table, 'lovely things! What's that? What's this? This one, for instance, this little sweet, do you see?' Vasya whispered, pointing to a charming cap further away, which was not the one he meant to buy, because he had already from afar descried and fixed his eyes upon the real, famous one, standing at the other end. He looked at it in such a way that one might have supposed someone was going to steal it, or as though the cap itself might take wings and fly into the air just to prevent Vasya from obtaining it.

'Look,' said Arkady Ivanovitch, pointing to one, 'I think that's better.'

'Well, Arkasha, that does you credit; I begin to respect you for your taste,' said Vasya, resorting to cunning with Arkasha in the tenderness of his heart, 'your cap is charming, but come this way.'

'Where is there a better one, brother?'

'Look; this way.'

'That,' said Arkady, doubtfully.

But when Vasya, incapable of restraining himself any longer, took it from the stand from which it seemed to fly spontaneously, as though delighted at falling at last into the hands of so good a customer, and they heard the rustle of its ribbons, ruches and lace, an unexpected cry of delight broke from the powerful chest of Arkady Ivanovitch. Even Madame Leroux, while maintaining her incontestable dignity and pre-eminence in matters of taste, and remaining mute from condescension, rewarded Vasya with a smile of complete approbation, everything in her glance, gesture and smile saying at once: 'Yes, you have chosen rightly, and are worthy of the happiness which awaits you.'

'It has been dangling its charms in coy seclusion,' cried Vasya, transferring his tender feelings to the charming cap. 'You have been hiding on purpose, you sly little pet!' And he kissed it, that is the air surrounding it, for he was afraid to touch his treasure.

'Retiring as true worth and virtue,' Arkady added enthusiastically, quoting humorously from a comic paper he had read that morning. 'Well, Vasya?'

'Hurrah, Arkasha! You are witty today. I predict you will make a sensation, as women say. Madame Leroux, Madame Leroux!'

'What is your pleasure?'

'Dear Madame Leroux.'

Madame Leroux looked at Arkady Ivanovitch and smiled condescendingly.

'You wouldn't believe how I adore you at this moment . . . Allow me to give you a kiss . . .' And Vasya kissed the shopkeeper.

She certainly at that moment needed all her dignity to maintain her position with such a madcap. But I contend that the innate, spontaneous courtesy and grace with which Madame Leroux received Vasya's enthusiasm, was equally befitting. She forgave him, and how tactfully, how graciously, she knew how to behave in the circumstances. How could she have been angry with Vasya?

'Madame Leroux, how much?'

'Five roubles in silver,' she answered, straightening herself with a new smile.

'And this one, Madame Leroux?' said Arkady Ivanovitch, pointing to his choice.

'That one is eight roubles.'

'There, you see — there, you see! Come, Madame Leroux, tell me which is nicer, more graceful, more charming, which of them suits you best?'

'The second is richer, but your choice *c'est plus coquet*.'

'Then we will take it.'

Madame Leroux took a sheet of very delicate paper, pinned it up, and the paper with the cap wrapped in it seemed even lighter than the paper alone. Vasya took it carefully, almost holding his breath, bowed to Madame Leroux, said something else very polite to her and left the shop.

'I am a lady's man, I was born to be a lady's man,' said Vasya, laughing a little noiseless, nervous laugh and dodging the passers-by, whom he suspected of designs for crushing his precious cap.

'Listen, Arkady, brother,' he began a minute later, and there was a note of triumph, of infinite affection in his voice. 'Arkady, I am so happy, I am so happy!'

'Vasya! how glad I am, dear boy!'

'No, Arkasha, no. I know that there is no limit to your affection for me; but you cannot be feeling one-hundredth part of what I am feeling at this moment. My heart is so full, so full! Arkasha, I am not worthy of such happiness. I feel that, I am conscious of it. Why has it come to me?' he said, his voice full of stifled sobs. 'What have I done to deserve it? Tell me. Look what lots of people, what lots of tears, what sorrow, what work-a-day life without a holiday, while I, I am loved by a girl like that, I . . . But you will see her yourself immediately, you will appreciate her noble heart. I was born in a humble station, now I have a grade in the service and an independent income – my salary. I was born with a physical defect, I am a little deformed. See, she loves me as I am. Yulian Mastakovitch was so kind, so attentive, so gracious today; he does not often talk to me; he came up to me: "Well, how goes it, Vasya" (yes, really, he called me Vasya), "are you going to have a good time for the holiday, eh?" he laughed.

' "Well, the fact is, Your Excellency, I have work to do," but then I plucked up courage and said: "and maybe I shall have a good time, too, Your Excellency." I really said it. He gave me the money, on the spot, then he said a couple of words more to me. Tears came into my eyes, brother, I actually cried, and he, too, seemed touched, he patted me on the shoulder, and said: "Feel always, Vasya, as you feel this now." '

Vasya paused for an instant. Arkady Ivanovitch turned away, and he, too, wiped away a tear with his fist.

'And, and . . .' Vasya went on, 'I have never spoken

to you of this, Arkady . . . Arkady, you make me so happy with your affection, without you I could not live – no, no, don't say anything, Arkady, let me squeeze your hand, let me . . . tha . . . ank . . . you . . .' Again Vasya could not finish.

Arkady Ivanovitch longed to throw himself on Vasya's neck, but as they were crossing the road and heard almost in their ears a shrill: 'Hi! there!' they ran frightened and excited to the pavement.

Arkady Ivanovitch was positively relieved. He set down Vasya's outburst of gratitude to the exceptional circumstances of the moment. He was vexed. He felt that he had done so little for Vasya hitherto. He felt actually ashamed of himself when Vasya began thanking him for so little. But they had all their lives before them, and Arkady Ivanovitch breathed more freely.

The Artemyevs had quite given up expecting them. The proof of it was that they had already sat down to tea! And the old, it seems, are sometimes more clear-sighted than the young, even when the young are so exceptional. Lizanka had very earnestly maintained, 'He isn't coming, he isn't coming, Mamma; I feel in my heart he is not coming;' while her mother on the contrary declared 'that she had a feeling that he would certainly come, that he would not stay away, that he would run round, that he could have no office work now, on New Year's Eve.' Even as Lizanka opened the door she did not in the least expect to see them, and greeted them breathlessly, with her heart throbbing like a captured bird's, flushing and turning as red as a cherry, a fruit which she wonderfully resembled. Good Heavens, what a surprise it was!

What a joyful 'Oh!' broke from her lips. 'Deceiver! My darling!' she cried, throwing her arms round Vasya's neck. But imagine her amazement, her sudden confusion: just behind Vasya, as though trying to hide behind his back, stood Arkady Ivanovitch, a trifle out of countenance. It must be admitted that he was awkward in the company of women, very awkward indeed, in fact on one occasion something occurred . . . but of that later. You must put yourself in his place, however. There was nothing to laugh at; he was standing in the entry, in his goloshes and overcoat, and in a cap with flaps over the ears, which he would have hastened to pull off, but he had, all twisted round in a hideous way, a yellow knitted scarf, which, to make things worse, was knotted at the back. He had to disentangle all this, to take it off as quickly as possible, to show himself to more advantage, for there is no one who does not prefer to show himself to advantage. And then Vasya, vexatious insufferable Vasya, of course always the same dear kind Vasya, but now insufferable, ruthless Vasya. 'Here,' he shouted, 'Lizanka, I have brought you my Arkady? What do you think of him? He is my best friend, embrace him, kiss him, Lizanka, give him a kiss in advance; afterwards – you will know him better – you can take it back again.'

Well, what, I ask you, was Arkady Ivanovitch to do? And he had only untwisted half of the scarf so far. I really am sometimes ashamed of Vasya's excess of enthusiasm; it is, of course, the sign of a good heart, but . . . it's awkward, not nice!

At last both went in . . . The mother was unutterably delighted to make Arkady Ivanovitch's acquaintance, 'she had heard so much about him, she had . . .' But she did not finish. A joyful 'Oh!' ringing musically through the room interrupted her in the middle of a sentence. Good Heavens! Lizanka was standing before the cap which had suddenly been unfolded before her gaze; she clasped her hands with the utmost simplicity, smiling such a smile . . . Oh, Heavens! why had not Madame Leroux an even lovelier cap?

Oh, Heavens! but where could you find a lovelier cap? It was quite first-rate. Where could you get a better one? I mean it seriously. This ingratitude on the part of lovers moves me, in fact, to indignation and even wounds me a little. Why, look at it for yourself, reader, look, what could be more beautiful than this little love of a cap? Come, look at it . . . But, no, no, my strictures are uncalled for; they had by now all agreed with me; it had been a momentary aberration; the blindness, the delirium of feeling; I am ready to forgive them . . . But then you must look . . . You must excuse me, kind reader, I am still talking about the cap: made of tulle, light as a feather, a broad cherry-coloured ribbon covered with lace passing between the tulle and the ruche, and at the back two wide long ribbons – they would fall down a little below the nape of the neck . . . All that the cap needed was to be tilted a little to the back of the head; come, look at it; I ask you, after that . . . but I see you are not looking . . . you think it does not matter. You are looking in a different direction . . . You are looking at two big tears, big as pearls, that rose in two jet black eyes, quivered for one instant on the eyelashes, and then dropped on the ethereal tulle of which Madame Leroux's artistic masterpiece was composed . . . And again I feel vexed, those two tears were scarcely a tribute to the cap . . . No, to my mind, such a gift should be given in cool blood, as only then can its full worth be appreciated. I am, I confess, dear reader, entirely on the side of the cap.

They sat down — Vasya with Lizanka and the old mother with Arkady Ivanovitch; they began to talk, and Arkady Ivanovitch did himself credit, I am glad to say that for him. One would hardly, indeed, have expected it of him. After a couple of words about Vasya he most successfully turned the conversation to Yulian Mastakovitch, his patron. And he talked so cleverly, so cleverly that the subject was not exhausted for an hour. You ought to have seen with what dexterity, what tact, Arkady Ivanovitch touched upon certain peculiarities of Yulian Mastakovitch which directly or indirectly affected Vasya. The mother was fascinated, genuinely fascinated; she admitted it herself; she purposely called Vasya aside, and said to him that his friend was a most excellent and charming young man, and, what was of most account, such a serious, steady young man. Vasya almost laughed aloud with delight. He remembered how the serious Arkady had tumbled him on his bed for a quarter of an hour. Then the mother signed to Vasya to follow her quietly and cautiously into the next room. It must be admitted that she treated Lizanka rather unfairly: she behaved treacherously to her daughter, in the fullness of her heart, of course, and showed Vasya on the sly the present Lizanka was preparing to give him for the New Year. It was a paper-case, embroidered in beads and gold in a very choice design: on one side was depicted a stag, absolutely lifelike, running swiftly, and so well done! On the other side was the portrait of a celebrated General, also an excellent likeness. I cannot describe Vasya's raptures. Meanwhile, time was not being wasted in the parlour. Lizanka went straight up to Arkady Ivanovitch. She took his hand, she thanked him for something, and Arkady Ivanovitch gathered that she was referring to her precious Vasya. Lizanka was, indeed, deeply touched: she had heard that Arkady Ivanovitch was such a true friend of her betrothed, so loved him, so watched over him, guiding him at every step with helpful advice, that she, Lizanka, could hardly help thanking him, could not refrain from feeling grateful, and hoping that Arkady Ivanovitch might like her, if only half as well as Vasya. Then she began questioning him as to whether Vasya was careful of his health, expressed some apprehensions in regard to his marked impulsiveness of character, and his lack of knowledge of men and practical life; she said that she would in time watch over him religiously, that she would take care of and cherish his lot, and finally, she hoped that Arkady Ivanovitch would not leave them, but would live with them.

'We three shall live like one,' she cried, with extremely naïve enthusiasm.

But it was time to go. They tried, of course, to keep them, but Vasya answered point blank that it was impossible. Arkady Ivanovitch said the same. The reason was, of course, inquired into, and it came out at once that there was work to be done entrusted to Vasya by Yulian Mastakovitch, urgent, necessary, dreadful work, which must be handed in on the morning of the next day but one, and that it was not only unfinished, but had been completely laid aside. The mamma sighed when she heard of this, while Lizanka was positively scared, and hurried Vasya off in alarm. The last kiss lost nothing from this haste; though brief and hurried it was only the more warm and ardent. At last they parted and the two friends set off home.

Both began at once confiding to each other their impressions as soon as they found themselves in the street. And could they help it? Indeed, Arkady Ivanovitch was in love, desperately in love, with Lizanka. And to whom could he better confide his feelings than to Vasya, the happy man himself. And so he did; he was not bashful, but confessed everything at once to Vasya. Vasya laughed heartily and was immensely delighted, and even observed that this was all that was needed to make them greater friends than ever. 'You have guessed my feelings, Vasya,' said Arkady Ivanovitch. 'Yes, I love her as I love you; she will be my good angel as well as yours, for the radiance of your happiness will be shed on me, too, and I can bask in its warmth. She will keep house for me too, Vasya; my happiness will be in her hands. Let her keep house for me as she will for you. Yes, friendship for you is friendship for her; you are not separable for me now, only I shall have two beings like you instead of one . . .' Arkady paused in the fullness of his feelings, while Vasya was shaken to the depths of his being by his friend's words. The fact is, he had never expected anything of the sort from Arkady. Arkady Ivanovitch was not very great at talking as a rule, he was not fond of dreaming, either; now he gave way to the liveliest, freshest, rainbow-tinted day-dreams. 'How I will protect and cherish you both,' he began again. 'To begin with, Vasya, I will be godfather to all your children, every one of them; and secondly, Vasya, we must bestir ourselves about the future. We must buy furniture, and take a lodging so that you and she and I can each have a little room to ourselves. Do you know, Vasya, I'll run about tomorrow and look at the notices, on the gates! Three . . . no, two rooms, we should not need more. I really believe, Vasya, I talked nonsense this morning, there will be money enough; why, as soon as I glanced into her eyes I calculated at once that there would be enough to live on. It will all be for her. Oh, how we will work! Now, Vasya, we might venture up to twenty-five roubles for rent. A lodging is everything, brother. Nice rooms . . . and at once a man is cheerful, and his dreams are of the brightest hues. And, besides, Lizanka will keep the purse for both of us: not a farthing will be wasted. Do you suppose I would go to a res-taurant? What do you take me for? Not on any account. And then we shall get a bonus and reward, for we shall be zealous in the service – oh! how we shall work, like oxen toiling in the fields . . . Only fancy,' and Arkady Ivanovitch's voice was faint with pleasure, 'all at once and quite unexpected, twenty-five or thirty roubles . . . Whenever there's an extra, there'll be a cap or a scarf or a pair of little stockings. She must knit me a scarf; look what a horrid one I've got, the nasty yellow thing, it did me a bad turn today! And you wore a nice one, Vasya, to introduce me while I had my head in a halter . . . Though never mind that now. And look here, I undertake all the silver. I am bound to give you some little present – that will be an honour, that will flatter my vanity . . . My bonuses won't fail me, surely; you don't suppose they would give them to Skorohodov? No fear, they won't be landed in that person's pocket. I'll buy you silver spoons, brother, good knives – not silver knives, but thoroughly good ones; and a waistcoat, that is a waistcoat for myself. I shall be best man, of course. Only now, brother, you must keep at it, you must keep at it. I shall stand over you with a stick, brother, today and tomorrow and all night; I shall worry you to work. Finish, make haste and finish, brother. And then again to spend the evening, and then again both of us happy; we will go in for loto. We will spend the evening there – oh, it's jolly! Oh, the devil! How, vexing it is I can't help you. I should like to take it and write it all for you . . . Why is it our handwriting is not alike?'

'Yes,' answered Vasya. 'Yes, I must make haste. I think it must be eleven o'clock; we must make haste . . . To work!' And saying this, Vasya, who had been all the time alternately smiling and trying to interrupt with some enthusiastic rejoinder the flow of his friend's feelings, and had, in short, been showing the most cordial response, suddenly subsided, sank into silence, and almost ran along the street. It seemed as though some burdensome idea had suddenly chilled his feverish head; he seemed all at once dispirited.

Arkady Ivanovitch felt quite uneasy; he scarcely got an answer to his hurried questions from Vasya, who confined himself to a word or two, sometimes an irrelevant exclamation.

'Why, what is the matter with you, Vasya?' he cried at last, hardly able to keep up with him. 'Can you really be so uneasy?'

'Oh, brother, that's enough chatter!' Vasya answered, with vexation.

'Don't be depressed, Vasya – come, come,' Arkady interposed. 'Why, I have known you write much more in a shorter time! What's the matter? You've simply a talent for it! You can write quickly in an emergency; they are not going to lithograph your copy. You've plenty of time! . . . The only thing is that you are excited now, and preoccupied, and the work won't go so easily.'

Vasya made no reply, or muttered something to himself, and they both ran home in genuine anxiety.

Vasya sat down to the papers at once. Arkady Ivanovitch was quiet and silent; he noiselessly undressed and went to bed, keeping his eyes fixed on Vasya . . . A sort of panic came over him . . . 'What is the matter with him?' he thought to himself, looking at Vasya's face that grew whiter and whiter, at his feverish eyes, at the anxiety that was betrayed in every movement he made, 'why, his hand is shaking . . . what a stupid! Why did I not advise him to sleep for a couple of hours, till he had slept off his nervous excitement, any way.' Vasya had just finished a page, he raised his eyes, glanced casually at Arkady and at once, looking down, took up his pen again.

'Listen, Vasya,' Arkady Ivanovitch began suddenly, 'wouldn't it be best to sleep a little now? Look, you are in a regular fever.'

Vasya glanced at Arkady with vexation, almost with anger, and made no answer.

'Listen, Vasya, you'll make yourself ill.'

Vasya at once changed his mind. 'How would it be to have tea, Arkady?' he said.

'How so? Why?'

'It will do me good. I am not sleepy, I'm not going to bed! I am going on writing. But now I should like to rest and have a cup of tea, and the worst moment will be over.'

'First-rate, brother Vasya, delightful! Just so. I was wanting to propose it myself. And I can't think why it did not occur to me to do so. But I say, Mavra won't get up, she won't wake for anything . . .'

'True.'

'That's no matter, though,' cried Arkady Ivanovitch, leaping out of bed. 'I will set the samovar myself. It won't be the first time . . .'

Arkady Ivanovitch ran to the kitchen and set to work to get the samovar; Vasya meanwhile went on writing. Arkady Ivanovitch, moreover, dressed and ran out to the baker's, so that Vasya might have something to sustain him for the night. A quarter of an hour later the samovar was on the table. They began drinking tea, but conversation flagged. Vasya still seemed preoccupied.

'Tomorrow,' he said at last, as though he had just thought of it, 'I shall have to take my congratulations for the New Year . . .'

'You need not go at all.'

'Oh yes, brother, I must,' said Vasya.

'Why, I will sign the visitors' book for you everywhere . . . How can you? You work tomorrow. You must work tonight, till five o'clock in the morning, as I said, and then get to bed. Or else you will be good for nothing tomorrow. I'll wake you at eight o'clock, punctually.'

'But will it be all right, your signing for me?' said Vasya, half assenting.

'Why, what could be better? Everyone does it.'

'I am really afraid.'

'Why, why?'

'It's all right, you know, with other people, but Yulian Mastakovitch . . . he has been so kind to me, you know, Arkasha, and when he notices it's not my own signature—'

'Notices! why, what a fellow you are, really, Vasya! How could he notice? . . . Come, you know I can imitate your signature awfully well, and make just the same flourish to it, upon my word I can. What nonsense! Who would notice?'

Vasya, made no reply, but emptied his glass hurriedly . . . Then he shook his head doubtfully.

'Vasya, dear boy! Ah, if only we succeed! Vasya, what's the matter with you, you quite frighten me! Do you know, Vasya, I am not going to bed now, I am not going to sleep! Show me, have you a great deal left?'

Vasya gave Arkady such a look that his heart sank, and his tongue failed him.

'Vasya, what is the matter? What are you thinking? Why do you look like that?'

'Arkady, I really must go tomorrow to wish Yulian Mastakovitch a happy New Year.'

'Well, go then!' said Arkady, gazing at him open-eyed, in uneasy expectation. 'I say, Vasya, do write faster;

I am advising you for your good, I really am! How often Yulian Mastakovitch himself has said that what he likes particularly about your writing is its legibility. Why, it is all that Skoroplehin cares for, that writing should be good and distinct like a copy, so as afterwards to pocket the paper and take it home for his children to copy; he can't buy copybooks, the blockhead! Yulian Mastakovitch is always saying, always insisting: "Legible, legible, legible!" . . . What is the matter? Vasya, I really don't know how to talk to you . . . it quite frightens me . . . you crush me with your depression.'

'It's all right, it's all right,' said Vasya, and he fell back in his chair as though fainting. Arkady was alarmed.

'Will you have some water? Vasya! Vasya!'

'Don't, don't,' said Vasya, pressing his hand. 'I am all right, I only feel sad, I can't tell why. Better talk of something else; let me forget it.'

'Calm yourself, for goodness' sake, calm yourself, Vasya. You will finish it all right, on my honour, you will. And even if you don't finish, what will it matter? You talk as though it were a crime!'

'Arkady,' said Vasya, looking at his friend with such meaning that Arkady was quite frightened, for Vasya had never been so agitated before . . . 'If I were alone, as I used to be . . . No! I don't mean that. I keep wanting to tell you as a friend, to confide in you . . . But why worry you, though? . . . You see, Arkady, to some much is given, others do a little thing as I do. Well, if gratitude, appreciation, is expected of you . . . and you can't give it?'

'Vasya, I don't understand you in the least.'

'I have never been ungrateful,' Vasya went on softly, as though speaking to himself, 'but if I am incapable of expressing all I feel, it seems as though . . . it seems, Arkady, as though I am really ungrateful, and that's killing me.'

'What next, what next! As though gratitude meant nothing more than your finishing that copy in time? Just think what you are saying, Vasya? Is that the whole expression of gratitude?'

Vasya sank into silence at once, and looked open-eyed at Arkady, as though his unexpected argument had settled all his doubts. He even smiled, but the same melancholy expression came back to his face at once. Arkady, taking this smile as a sign that all his uneasiness was over, and the look that succeeded it as an indication that he was determined to do better, was greatly relieved.

'Well, brother Arkasha, you will wake up,' said Vasya, 'keep an eye on me; if I fall asleep it will be dreadful. I'll set to work now . . . Arkasha?'

'What?'

'Oh, it's nothing, I only . . . I meant . . .'

Vasya settled himself, and said no more, Arkady got into bed. Neither of them said one word about their friends, the Artemyevs. Perhaps both of them felt that they had been a little to blame, and that they ought not to have gone for their jaunt when they did. Arkady soon fell asleep, still worried about Vasya. To his own surprise he woke up exactly at eight o'clock in the morning. Vasya was asleep in his chair with the pen in his hand, pale and exhausted; the candle had burnt out. Mavra was busy getting the samovar ready in the kitchen.

'Vasya, Vasya!' Arkady cried in alarm, 'when did you fall asleep?'

Vasya opened his eyes and jumped up from his chair.

'Oh!' he cried, 'I must have fallen asleep . . .'

He flew to the papers – everything was right; all were in order; there was not a blot of ink, nor spot of grease from the candle on them.

'I think I must have fallen asleep about six o'clock,' said Vasya. 'How cold it is in the night! Let us have tea, and I will go on again . . .'

'Do you feel better?'

'Yes, yes, I'm all right, I'm all right now.'

'A happy New Year to you, brother Vasya.'

'And to you too, brother, the same to you, dear boy.'

They embraced each other. Vasya's chin was quivering and his eyes were moist. Arkady Ivanovitch was silent, he felt sad. They drank their tea hastily.

'Arkady, I've made up my mind, I am going myself to Yulian Mastakovitch.'

'Why, he wouldn't notice—'

'But my conscience feels ill at ease, brother.'

'But you know it's for his sake you are sitting here; it's for his sake you are wearing yourself out.'

'Enough!'

'Do you know what, brother, I'll go round and see . . .'

'Whom?' asked Vasya.

'The Artemyevs. I'll take them your good wishes for the New Year as well as mine.'

'My dear fellow! Well, I'll stay here; and I see it's a

good idea of yours; I shall be working here, I shan't waste my time. Wait one minute, I'll write a note.'

'Yes, do brother, do, there's plenty of time. I've still to wash and shave and to brush my best coat. Well, Vasya, we are going to be contented and happy. Embrace me, Vasya.'

'Ah, if only we may, brother . . .'

'Does Mr Shumkov live here?' they heard a child's voice on the stairs.

'Yes, my dear, yes,' said Mavra, showing the visitor in.

'What's that? What is it?' cried Vasya, leaping up from the table and rushing to the entry, 'Petinka, you?'

'Good morning, I have the honour to wish you a happy New Year, Vassily Petrovitch,' said a pretty boy of ten years old with curly black hair. 'Sister sends you her love, and so does Mamma, and Sister told me to give you a kiss for her.'

Vasya caught the messenger up in the air and printed a long, enthusiastic kiss on his lips, which were very much like Lizanka's.

'Kiss him, Arkady,' he said handing Petya to him, and without touching the ground the boy was transferred to Arkady Ivanovitch's powerful and eager arms.

'Will you have some breakfast, dear?'

'Thank you, very much. We have had it already, we got up early today, the others have gone to church. Sister was two hours curling my hair, and pomading it, washing me and mending my trousers, for I tore them yesterday, playing with Sashka in the street, we were snowballing.'

'Well, well, well!'

'So she dressed me up to come and see you, and then pomaded my head and then gave me a regular kissing. She said: "Go to Vasya, wish him a happy New Year, and ask whether they are happy, whether they had a good night, and . . ." to ask something else — oh yes! whether you had finished the work you spoke of yesterday . . . when you were there. Oh, I've got it all written down,' said the boy, reading from a slip of paper which he took out of his pocket. 'Yes, they were uneasy.'

'It will be finished! It will be! Tell her that it will be. I shall finish it, on my word of honour!'

'And something else . . . Oh yes, I forgot. Sister sent a little note and a present, and I was forgetting it! . . .'

'My goodness! Oh, you little darling! Where is it? where is it? That's it, oh! Look, brother, see what she writes. The dar — ling, the precious! You know I saw there yesterday a paper-case for me; it's not finished, so she says, "I am sending you a lock of my hair, and the other will come later." Look, brother, look!'

And overwhelmed with rapture he showed Arkady Ivanovitch a curl of luxuriant, jet-black hair; then he kissed it fervently and put it in his breast pocket, nearest his heart.

'Vasya, I shall get you a locket for that curl,' Arkady Ivanovitch said resolutely at last.

'And we are going to have hot veal, and tomorrow brains. Mamma wants to make cakes . . . but we are not going to have millet porridge,' said the boy, after a moment's thought, to wind up his budget of interesting items.

'Oh! what a pretty boy,' cried Arkady Ivanovitch. 'Vasya, you are the happiest of mortals.'

The boy finished his tea, took from Vasya a note, a thousand kisses, and went out happy and frolicsome as before.

'Well, brother,' began Arkady Ivanovitch, highly delighted, 'you see how splendid it all is; you see. Everything is going well, don't be downcast, don't be uneasy. Go ahead! Get it done, Vasya, get it done. I'll be home at two o'clock. I'll go round to them, and then to Yulian Mastakovitch.'

'Well, goodbye, brother; goodbye . . . Oh! if only . . . Very good, you go, very good,' said Vasya, 'then I really won't go to Yulian Mastakovitch.'

'Goodbye.'

'Stay, brother, stay, tell them . . . well, whatever you think fit. Kiss her . . . and give me a full account of everything afterwards.'

'Come, come – of course, I know all about it. This happiness has upset you. The suddenness of it all; you've not been yourself since yesterday. You have not got over the excitement of yesterday. Well, it's settled. Now try and get over it, Vasya. Goodbye, goodbye!'

At last the friends parted. All the morning Arkady Ivanovitch was preoccupied, and could think of nothing but Vasya. He knew his weak, highly nervous character. 'Yes, this happiness has upset him, I was right there,' he said to himself. 'Upon my word, he has made me quite depressed, too, that man will make a tragedy of anything! What a feverish creature! Oh, I must save him! I must save him!' said Arkady, not noticing that he himself was exaggerating into something serious a slight trouble, in reality quite trivial. Only at eleven o'clock he reached the porter's lodge of Yulian Mastakovitch's house, to add his modest name to the long list of illustrious persons who had written their names on a sheet of blotted and scribbled paper in the porter's lodge. What was his surprise when he saw just above his own the signature of Vasya Shumkov! It amazed him. 'What's the matter with him?' he thought. Arkady Ivanovitch, who had just been so buoyant with hope, came out feeling upset. There was certainly going to be trouble, but how? And in what form?

He reached the Artemyevs with gloomy forebodings; he seemed absent-minded from the first, and after talking a little with Lizanka went away with tears in his eyes; he was really anxious about Vasya. He went home running, and on the Neva came full tilt upon Vasya himself. The latter, too, was uneasy.

'Where are you going?' cried Arkady Ivanovitch.

Vasya stopped as though he had been caught in a crime.

'Oh, it's nothing, brother, I wanted to go for a walk.'

'You could not stand it, and have been to the Artemyevs? Oh, Vasya, Vasya! Why did you go to Yulian Mastakovitch?'

Vasya did not answer, but then with a wave of his hand, he said: 'Arkady, I don't know what is the matter with me. I . . .'

'Come, come, Vasya. I know what it is. Calm yourself. You've been excited, and overwrought ever since yesterday. Only think, it's not much to bear. Everybody's fond of you, everybody's ready to do anything for you; your work is getting on all right; you will get it done, you will certainly get it done. I know that you have been imagining something, you have had apprehensions about something . . .'

'No, it's all right, it's all right . . .'

'Do you remember, Vasya, do you remember it was the same with you once before; do you remember, when you got your promotion, in your joy and thankfulness you were so zealous that you spoilt all your work for a week? It is just the same with you now.'

'Yes, yes, Arkady; but now it is different, it is not that at all.'

'How is it different? And very likely the work is not urgent at all, while you are killing yourself . . .'

'It's nothing, it's nothing. I am all right, it's nothing. Well, come along!'

'Why, are you going home, and not to them?'

'Yes, brother, how could I have the face to turn up there? . . . I have changed my mind. It was only that I could not stay on alone without you; now you are coming back with me I'll sit down to write again. Let us go!'

They walked along and for some time were silent. Vasya was in haste.

'Why don't you ask me about them?' said Arkady Ivanovitch.

'Oh, yes! Well, Arkasha, what about them?'

'Vasya, you are not like yourself.'

'Oh, I am all right, I am all right. Tell me everything, Arkasha,' said Vasya, in an imploring voice, as though to avoid further explanations. Arkady Ivanovitch sighed. He felt utterly at a loss, looking at Vasya.

III

His account of their friends roused Vasya. He even grew talkative. They had dinner together. Lizanka's mother had filled Arkady Ivanovitch's pockets with little cakes, and eating them the friends grew more cheerful. After dinner Vasya promised to take a nap, so as to sit up all night. He did, in fact, lie down. In the morning, some one whom it was impossible to refuse had invited Arkady Ivanovitch to tea. The friends parted. Arkady promised to come back as soon as he could, by eight o'clock if possible. The three hours of separation seemed to him like three years. At last he got away and rushed back to Vasya. When he went into the room, he found it in darkness. Vasya was not at home. He asked Mavra. Mavra said that he had been writing all the time, and had not slept at all, then he had paced up and down the room, and after that, an hour before, he had run out, saying he would be back in half-an-hour; 'and when, says he, Arkady Ivanovitch comes in, tell him, old woman, says he,' Mavra told him in conclusion, 'that I have gone out for a walk,' and he repeated the order three or four times.

'He is at the Artemyevs,' thought Arkady Ivanovitch, and he shook his head.

A minute later he jumped up with renewed hope.

'He has simply finished,' he thought, 'that's all it is; he couldn't wait, but ran off there. But, no! he would have waited for me . . . Let's have a peep what he has there.'

He lighted a candle, and ran to Vasya's writing-table: the work had made progress and it looked as though there were not much left to do. Arkady Ivanovitch was about to investigate further, when Vasya himself walked in . . .

'Oh, you are here?' he cried, with a start of dismay.

Arkady Ivanovitch was silent. He was afraid to question Vasya. The latter dropped his eyes and remained silent too, as he began sorting the papers. At last their eyes met. The look in Vasya's was so beseeching, imploring, and broken, that Arkady shuddered when he saw it. His heart quivered and was full.

'Vasya, my dear boy, what is it? What's wrong?' he cried, rushing to him and squeezing him in his arms. 'Explain to me, I don't understand you, and your depression. What is the matter with you, my poor, tormented boy? What is it? Tell me all about it, without hiding anything. It can't be only this—'

Vasya held him tight and could say nothing. He could scarcely breathe.

'Don't, Vasya, don't! Well, if you don't finish it, what then? I don't understand you; tell me your trouble. You see it is for your sake I . . . Oh dear! oh dear!' he said, walking up and down the room and clutching at everything he came across, as though seeking at once some remedy for Vasya. 'I will go to Yulian Mastakovitch instead of you tomorrow. I will ask him – entreat him – to let you have another day. I will explain it all to him, anything, if it worries you so . . .'

'God forbid!' cried Vasya, and turned as white as the wall. He could scarcely stand on his feet.

'Vasya! Vasya!'

Vasya pulled himself together. His lips were quivering; he tried to say something, but could only convulsively squeeze Arkady's hand in silence. His hand was cold. Arkady stood facing him, full of anxious and miserable suspense. Vasya raised his eyes again.

'Vasya, God bless you, Vasya! You wring my heart, my dear boy, my friend.'

Tears gushed from Vasya's eyes; he flung himself on Arkady's bosom.

'I have deceived you, Arkady,' he said. 'I have deceived you. Forgive me, forgive me! I have been faithless to your friendship . . .'

'What is it, Vasya? What is the matter?' asked Arkady, in real alarm.

'Look!'

And with a gesture of despair Vasya tossed out of the drawer on to the table six thick manuscripts, similar to the one he had copied.

'What's this?'

'What I have to get through by the day after to-morrow. I haven't done a quarter! Don't ask me, don't ask me how it has happened,' Vasya went on, speaking at once of what was distressing him so terribly. 'Arkady, dear friend, I don't know myself what came over me. I feel as though I were coming out of a dream. I have wasted three weeks doing nothing. I kept . . . I . . . kept going to see her . . . My heart was aching, I was tormented by . . . the uncertainty . . . I could not write. I did not even think about it. Only now, when happiness is at hand for me, I have come to my senses.'

'Vasya,' began Arkady Ivanovitch resolutely, 'Vasya, I will save you. I understand it all. It's a serious matter; I will save you. Listen! listen to me: I will go to Yulian

Mastakovitch tomorrow . . . Don't shake your head; no, listen! I will tell him exactly how it has all been; let me do that . . . I will explain to him . . . I will go into everything. I will tell him how crushed you are, how you are worrying yourself.'

'Do you know that you are killing me now?' Vasya brought out, turning cold with horror.

Arkady Ivanovitch turned pale, but at once controlling himself, laughed.

'Is that all? Is that all?' he said. 'Upon my word, Vasya, upon my word! Aren't you ashamed? Come, listen! I see that I am grieving you. You see I understand you; I know what is passing in your heart. Why, we have been living together for five years, thank God! You are such a kind, soft-hearted fellow, but weak, unpardonably weak. Why, even Lizaveta Mikalovna has noticed it. And you are a dreamer, and that's a bad thing, too; you may go from bad to worse, brother. I tell you, I know what you want! You would like Yulian Mastakovitch, for instance, to be beside himself and, maybe, to give a ball, too, from joy, because you are going to get married . . . Stop, stop! you are frowning. You see that at one word from me you are offended on Yulian Mastakovitch's account. I'll let him alone. You know I respect him just as much as you do. But argue as you may, you can't prevent my thinking that you would like there to be no one unhappy in the whole world when you are getting married . . . Yes, brother, you must admit that you would like me, for instance, your best friend, to come in for a fortune of a hundred thousand all of a sudden, you would like all the enemies in the world to be suddenly, for no rhyme or reason, reconciled, so that in their joy they might all embrace one another in the middle of the street, and then, perhaps, come here to call on you. Vasya, my dear boy, I am not laughing; it is true; you've said as much to me long ago, in different ways. Because you are happy, you want everyone, absolutely everyone, to become happy at once. It hurts you and troubles you to be happy alone. And so you want at once to do your utmost to be worthy of that happiness, and maybe to do some great deed to satisfy your conscience. Oh! I understand how ready you are to distress yourself for having suddenly been remiss just where you ought to have shown your zeal, your capacity . . . well, maybe your gratitude, as you say. It is very bitter for you to think that Yulian Mastak-ovitch may frown and even be angry when he sees that you have not justified the expectations he had of you. It hurts you to think that you may hear reproaches from the man you look upon as your benefactor – and at such a moment! when your heart is full of joy and you don't know on whom to lavish your gratitude . . . Isn't that true? It is, isn't it?'

Arkady Ivanovitch, whose voice was trembling, paused, and drew a deep breath.

Vasya looked affectionately at his friend. A smile passed over his lips. His face even lighted up, as though with a gleam of hope.

'Well, listen, then,' Arkady Ivanovitch began again, growing more hopeful, 'there's no necessity that you should forfeit Yulian Mastakovitch's favour . . . Is there, dear boy? Is there any question of it? And since it is so,' said Arkady, jumping up, 'I shall sacrifice myself for you.

I am going tomorrow to Yulian Mastakovitch, and don't oppose me. You magnify your failure to a crime, Vasya. Yulian Mastakovitch is magnanimous and merciful, and, what is more, he is not like you. He will listen to you and me, and get us out of our trouble, brother Vasya. Well, are you calmer?'

Vasya pressed his friend's hands with tears in his eyes.

'Hush, hush, Arkady,' he said, 'the thing is settled. I haven't finished, so very well; if I haven't finished, I haven't finished, and there's no need for you to go. I will tell him all about it, I will go myself. I am calmer now, I am perfectly calm; only you mustn't go . . . But listen . . .'

'Vasya, my dear boy,' Arkady Ivanovitch cried joyfully, 'I judged from what you said. I am glad that you have thought better of things and have recovered yourself. But whatever may befall you, whatever happens, I am with you, remember that. I see that it worries you to think of my speaking to Yulian Mastakovitch – and I won't say a word, not a word, you shall tell him yourself. You see, you shall go tomorrow . . . Oh no, you had better not go, you'll go on writing here, you see, and I'll find out about this work, whether it is very urgent or not, whether it must be done by the time or not, and if you don't finish it in time what will come of it. Then I will run back to you. Do you see, do you see! There is still hope; suppose the work is not urgent – it may be all right. Yulian Mastakovitch may not remember, then all is saved.'

Vasya shook his head doubtfully. But his grateful eyes never left his friend's face.

'Come, that's enough, I am so weak, so tired,' he said, sighing. 'I don't want to think about it. Let us talk of something else. I won't write either now; do you know I'll only finish two short pages just to get to the end of a passage. Listen . . . I have long wanted to ask you, how is it you know me so well?'

Tears dropped from Vasya's eyes on Arkady's hand.

'If you knew, Vasya, how fond I am of you, you would not ask that – yes!'

'Yes, yes, Arkady, I don't know that, because I don't know why you are so fond of me. Yes, Arkady, do you know, even your love has been killing me? Do you know, ever so many times, particularly when I am thinking of you in bed (for I always think of you when I am falling asleep), I shed tears, and my heart throbs at the thought . . . at the thought . . . Well, at the thought that you are so fond of me, while I can do nothing to relieve my heart, can do nothing to repay you.'

'You see, Vasya, you see what a fellow you are! Why, how upset you are now,' said Arkady, whose heart ached at that moment and who remembered the scene in the street the day before.

'Nonsense, you want me to be calm, but I never have been so calm and happy! Do you know . . . Listen, I want to tell you all about it, but I am afraid of wounding you . . . You keep scolding me and being vexed; and I am afraid . . . See how I am trembling now, I don't know why. You see, this is what I want to say. I feel as though I had never known myself before – yes! Yes, I only began to understand other people too, yesterday. I did not feel or appreciate things fully, brother. My heart . . . was hard . . . Listen how has it happened, that I have never done good to anyone, anyone in the world, because I couldn't – I am not even pleasant to look at . . . But everybody does me good! You, to begin with: do you suppose I don't see that? Only I said nothing; only I said nothing.'

'Hush, Vasya!'

'Oh, Arkasha! . . . it's all right,' Vasya interrupted, hardly able to articulate for tears. 'I talked to you yesterday about Yulian Mastakovitch. And you know yourself how stern and severe he is, even you have come in for a reprimand from him; yet he deigned to jest with me yesterday, to show his affection, and kind-heartedness, which he prudently conceals from everyone . . .'

'Come, Vasya, that only shows you deserve your good fortune.'

'Oh, Arkasha! How I longed to finish all this . . . No, I shall ruin my good luck! I feel that! Oh no, not through that,' Vasya added, seeing that Arkady glanced at the heap of urgent work lying on the table, 'that's nothing, that's only paper covered with writing . . . it's nonsense! That matter's settled . . . I went to see them today, Arkasha; I did not go in. I felt depressed and sad. I simply stood at the door. She was playing the piano, I listened. You see, Arkady,' he went on, dropping his voice, 'I did not dare to go in.'

'I say, Vasya – what is the matter with you? You look at one so strangely.'

'Oh, it's nothing, I feel a little sick; my legs are trembling; it's because I sat up last night. Yes! Everything looks green before my eyes. It's here, here—'

He pointed to his heart. He fainted. When he came to himself Arkady tried to take forcible measures. He tried to compel him to go to bed. Nothing would induce Vasya to consent. He shed tears, wrung his hands, wanted to write, was absolutely set on finishing his two pages. To avoid exciting him Arkady let him sit down to the work.

'Do you know,' said Vasya, as he settled himself in his place, 'an idea has occurred to me? There is hope.'

He smiled to Arkady, and his pale face lighted up with a gleam of hope.

'I will take him what is done the day after tomorrow. About the rest I will tell a lie. I will say it has been burnt, that it has been sopped in water, that I have lost it . . . That, in fact, I have not finished it; I cannot lie. I will explain, do you know, what? I'll explain to him all about it. I will tell him how it was that I could not. I'll tell him about my love; he has got married himself just lately, he'll understand me. I will do it all, of course, respect-fully, quietly; he will see my tears and be touched by them . . .'

'Yes, of course, you must go, you must go and explain to him . . . But there's no need of tears! Tears for what? Really, Vasya, you quite scare me.'

'Yes, I'll go, I'll go. But now let me write, let me write, Arkasha. I am not interfering with anyone, let me write!'

Arkady flung himself on the bed. He had no confi-dence in Vasya, no confidence at all. 'Vasya was capable of anything, but to ask forgiveness for what? how? That was not the point. The point was, that Vasya had not carried out his obligations, that Vasya felt guilty *in his own eyes*, felt that he was ungrateful to destiny, that Vasya was crushed, overwhelmed by happiness and thought himself unworthy of it; that, in fact, he was simply trying to find an excuse to go off his head on that point, and that he had not recovered from the unexpectedness of what had happened the day before; that's what it is,' thought Arkady Ivanovitch. 'I must save him. I must reconcile him to himself. He will be his own ruin.' He thought and thought, and resolved to go at once next day to Yulian Mastakovitch, and to tell him all about it.

Vasya was sitting writing. Arkady Ivanovitch, worn out, lay down to think things over again, and only woke at daybreak.

'Damnation! Again!' he cried, looking at Vasya; the latter was still sitting writing.

Arkady rushed up to him, seized him and forcibly put him to bed. Vasya was smiling: his eyes were closing with sleep. He could hardly speak.

'I wanted to go to bed,' he said. 'Do you know, Arkady, I have an idea; I shall finish. I made my pen go faster! I could not have sat at it any longer; wake me at eight o'clock.'

Without finishing his sentence, he dropped asleep and slept like the dead.

'Mavra,' said Arkady Ivanovitch to Mavra, who came in with the tea, 'he asked to be waked in an hour. Don't wake him on any account! Let him sleep ten hours, if he can. Do you understand?'

'I understand, sir.'

'Don't get the dinner, don't bring in the wood, don't make a noise or it will be the worse for you. If he asks for me, tell him I have gone to the office – do you understand?'

'I understand, bless you, sir; let him sleep and welcome! I am glad my gentlemen should sleep well, and I take good care of their things. And about that cup that was broken, and you blamed me, your honour, it wasn't me, it was poor pussy broke it, I ought to have kept an eye on her. "S-sh, you confounded thing," I said.'

'Hush, be quiet, be quiet!'

Arkady Ivanovitch followed Mavra out into the kitchen, asked for the key and locked her up there. Then he went to the office. On the way he considered how he could present himself before Yulian Mastakovitch, and whether it would be appropriate and not impertinent. He went into the office timidly, and timidly inquired whether His Excellency were there; receiving the answer that he was not and would not be, Arkady Ivanovitch instantly thought of going to his flat, but reflected very prudently that if Yulian Mastakovitch had not come to the office he would certainly be busy at home. He remained. The hours seemed to him endless. Indirectly he inquired about the work entrusted to Shumkov, but no one knew anything about this. All that was known was that Yulian Mastakovitch did employ him on special jobs, but what they were – no one could say. At last it struck three o'clock, and Arkady Ivanovitch rushed out, eager to get home. In the vestibule he was met by a clerk, who told him that Vassily Petrovitch Shumkov had come about one o'clock and asked, the clerk added, 'whether you were here, and whether Yulian Mastakovitch had been here.' Hearing this Arkady Ivanovitch took a sledge and hastened home beside himself with alarm.

Shumkov was at home. He was walking about the room in violent excitement. Glancing at Arkady Ivanovitch, he immediately controlled himself, reflected, and hastened to conceal his emotion. He sat down to his papers without a word. He seemed to avoid his friend's questions, seemed to be bothered by them, to be pondering to himself on some plan, and deciding to conceal his decision, because he could not reckon further on his friend's affection. This struck Arkady, and his heart ached with a poignant and oppressive pain. He sat on the bed and began turning over the leaves of some book, the only one he had in his possession, keeping his eye on poor Vasya. But Vasya remained obstinately silent, writing, and not raising his head. So passed several hours, and Arkady's misery reached an extreme point. At last, at eleven o'clock, Vasya lifted his head and looked with a fixed, vacant stare at Arkady. Arkady waited. Two or three minutes passed; Vasya did not speak.

'Vasya!' cried Arkady.

Vasya made no answer.

'Vasya!' he repeated, jumping up from the bed, 'Vasya, what is the matter with you? What is it?' he cried, running up to him.

Vasya raised his eyes and again looked at him with the same vacant, fixed stare.

'He's in a trance!' thought Arkady, trembling all over with fear. He seized a bottle of water, raised Vasya, poured some water on his head, moistened his temples, rubbed his hands in his own – and Vasya came to himself.

'Vasya, Vasya!' cried Arkady, unable to restrain his tears. 'Vasya, save yourself, rouse yourself, rouse yourself! . . .' He could say no more, but held him tight in his arms. A look as of some oppressive sensation passed over Vasya's face; he rubbed his forehead and clutched at his head, as though he were afraid it would burst.

'I don't know what is the matter with me,' he added, at last. 'I feel torn to pieces. Come, it's all right, it's all right! Give over, Arkady; don't grieve,' he repeated, looking at him with sad, exhausted eyes. 'Why be so anxious? Come!'

'You, you comforting me!' cried Arkady, whose heart was torn. 'Vasya,' he said at last, 'lie down and have a little nap, won't you? Don't wear yourself out for nothing! You'll set to work better afterwards.'

'Yes, yes,' said Vasya, 'by all means, I'll lie down, very good. Yes! you see I meant to finish, but now I've changed my mind, yes . . .'

And Arkady led him to the bed.

'Listen, Vasya,' he said firmly, 'we must settle this matter finally. Tell me what were you thinking about?'

'Oh!' said Vasya, with a flourish of his weak hand turning over on the other side.

'Come, Vasya, come, make up your mind. I don't want to hurt you. I can't be silent any longer. You won't sleep till you've made up your mind, I know.'

'As you like, as you like,' Vasya repeated enigmatically.

'He will give in,' thought Arkady Ivanovitch.

'Attend to me, Vasya,' he said, 'remember what I say, and I will save you tomorrow; tomorrow I will decide your fate! What am I saying, your fate? You have so frightened me, Vasya, that I am using your own words. Fate, indeed! It's simply nonsense, rubbish! You don't want to lose Yulian Mastakovitch's favour — affection, if you like. No! And you won't lose it, you will see. I—'

Arkady Ivanovitch would have said more, but Vasya interrupted him. He sat up in bed, put both arms round Arkady Ivanovitch's neck and kissed him.

'Enough,' he said in a weak voice, 'enough! Say no more about that!'

And again he turned his face to the wall.

'My goodness!' thought Arkady, 'my goodness! What is the matter with him? He is utterly lost. What has he in his mind! He will be his own undoing.'

Arkady looked at him in despair.

'If he were to fall ill,' thought Arkady, 'perhaps it would be better. His trouble would pass off with illness, and that might be the best way of settling the whole business. But what nonsense I am talking. Oh, my God!'

Meanwhile Vasya seemed to be asleep. Arkady Ivanovitch was relieved. 'A good sign,' he thought. He made up his mind to sit beside him all night. But Vasya was restless; he kept twitching and tossing about on the bed, and opening his eyes for an instant. At last exhaustion got the upper hand, he slept like the dead. It was about two o'clock in the morning, Arkady Ivanovitch began to doze in the chair with his elbow on the table!

He had a strange and agitated dream. He kept fancying that he was not asleep, and that Vasya was still lying on the bed. But strange to say, he fancied that Vasya was pretending, that he was deceiving him, that he was getting up, stealthily watching him out of the corner of his eye, and was stealing up to the writing table. Arkady felt a scalding pain at his heart; he felt vexed and sad and oppressed to see Vasya not trusting him, hiding and concealing himself from him. He tried to catch hold of him, to call out, to carry him to the bed. Then Vasya kept shrieking in his arms, and he laid on the bed a lifeless corpse. He opened his eyes and woke up; Vasya was sitting before him at the table, writing.

Hardly able to believe his senses, Arkady glanced at the bed; Vasya was not there. Arkady jumped up in a panic, still under the influence of his dream. Vasya did not stir; he went on writing. All at once Arkady noticed with horror that Vasya was moving a dry pen over the paper, was turning over perfectly blank pages, and hurrying, hurrying to fill up the paper as though he were doing his work in a most thorough and efficient way. 'No, this is not a trance,' thought Arkady Ivanovitch, and he trembled all over.

'Vasya, Vasya, speak to me,' he cried, clutching him by the shoulder. But Vasya did not speak; he went on as before, scribbling with a dry pen over the paper.

'At last I have made the pen go faster,' he said, without looking up at Arkady.

Arkady seized his hand and snatched away the pen.

A moan broke from Vasya. He dropped his hand and raised his eyes to Arkady; then with an air of misery and exhaustion he passed his hand over his forehead as though he wanted to shake off some leaden weight that was pressing upon his whole being, and slowly, as though lost in thought, he let his head sink on his breast.

'Vasya, Vasya!' cried Arkady in despair. 'Vasya!'

A minute later Vasya looked at him, tears stood in his large blue eyes, and his pale, mild face wore a look of infinite suffering. He whispered something.

'What, what is it?' cried Arkady, bending down to him.

'What for, why are they doing it to me?' whispered Vasya. 'What for? What have I done?'

'Vasya, what is it? What are you afraid of? What is it?' cried Arkady, wringing his hands in despair.

'Why are they sending me for a soldier?' said Vasya, looking his friend straight in the face. 'Why is it? What have I done?'

Arkady's hair stood on end with horror; he refused to believe his ears. He stood over him, half dead.

A minute later he pulled himself together. 'It's nothing, it's only for the minute,' he said to himself, with pale face and blue, quivering lips, and he hastened to put on his outdoor things. He meant to run straight for a doctor. All at once Vasya called to him. Arkady rushed to him and clasped him in his arms like a mother whose child is being torn from her.

'Arkady, Arkady, don't tell anyone! Don't tell anyone, do you hear? It is my trouble, I must bear it alone.'

'What is it – what is it? Rouse yourself, Vasya, rouse yourself!'

Vasya sighed, and slow tears trickled down his cheeks.

'Why kill her? How is she to blame?' he muttered in an agonised, heartrending voice. 'The sin is mine, the sin is mine!'

He was silent for a moment.

'Farewell, my love! Farewell, my love!' he whispered,

shaking his luckless head. Arkady started, pulled himself together and would have rushed for the doctor. 'Let us go, it is time,' cried Vasya, carried away by Arkady's last movement. 'Let us go, brother, let us go; I am ready. You lead the way.' He paused and looked at Arkady with a downcast and mistrustful face.

'Vasya, for goodness' sake, don't follow me! Wait for me here. I will come back to you directly, directly,' said Arkady Ivanovitch, losing his head and snatching up his cap to run for a doctor. Vasya sat down at once, he was quiet and docile; but there was a gleam of some desperate resolution in his eye. Arkady turned back, snatched up from the table an open penknife, looked at the poor fellow for the last time, and ran out of the flat.

It was eight o'clock. It had been broad daylight for some time in the room.

He found no one. He was running about for a full hour. All the doctors whose addresses he had got from the house porter when he inquired of the latter whether there were no doctor living in the building, had gone out, either to their work or on their private affairs. There was one who saw patients. This one questioned at length and in detail the servant who announced that Nefedevitch had called, asking him who it was, from whom he came, what was the matter, and concluded by saying that he could not go, that he had a great deal to do, and that patients of that kind ought to be taken to a hospital.

Then Arkady, exhausted, agitated, and utterly taken aback by this turn of affairs, cursed all the doctors on earth, and rushed home in the utmost alarm about Vasya. He ran into the flat. Mavra, as though there were nothing the matter, went on scrubbing the floor, breaking up wood and preparing to light the stove. He went into the room; there was no trace of Vasya, he had gone out.

'Which way? Where? Where will the poor fellow be off to?' thought Arkady, frozen with terror. He began questioning Mavra. She knew nothing, had neither seen nor heard him go out, God bless him! Nefedevitch rushed off to the Artemyevs'.

It occurred to him for some reason that he must be there.

It was ten o'clock by the time he arrived. They did not expect him, knew nothing and had heard nothing. He stood before them frightened, distressed, and asked where was Vasya? The mother's legs gave way under her; she sank back on the sofa. Lizanka, trembling with alarm, began asking what had happened. What could he say? Arkady Ivanovitch got out of it as best he could, invented some tale which of course was not believed, and fled, leaving them distressed and anxious. He flew to his department that he might not be too late there, and he let them know that steps might be taken at once. On the way it occurred to him that Vasya would be at Yulian Mastakovitch's. That was more likely than anything: Arkady had thought of that first of all, even before the Artemyevs'. As he drove by His Excellency's door, he thought of stopping, but at once told the driver to go straight on. He made up his mind to try and find out whether anything had happened at the office, and if he were not there to go to His Excellency, ostensibly to report on Vasya. Some one must be informed of it.

As soon as he got into the waiting-room he was

surrounded by fellow-clerks, for the most part young men of his own standing in the service. With one voice they began asking him what had happened to Vasya? At the same time they all told him that Vasya had gone out of his mind, and thought that he was to be sent for a soldier as a punishment for having neglected his work. Arkady Ivanovitch, answering them in all directions, or rather avoiding giving a direct answer to anyone, rushed into the inner room. On the way he learned that Vasya was in Yulian Mastakovitch's private room, that everyone had been there and that Esper Ivanovitch had gone in there too. He was stopped on the way. One of the senior clerks asked him who he was and what he wanted? Without distinguishing the person he said something about Vasya and went straight into the room. He heard Yulian Mastakovitch's voice from within. 'Where are you going?' some one asked him at the very door. Arkady Ivanovitch was almost in despair; he was on the point of turning back, but through the open door he saw his poor Vasya. He pushed the door and squeezed his way into the room. Everyone seemed to be in confusion and perplexity, because Yulian Mastakovitch was apparently much chagrined. All the more important personages were standing about him talking, and coming to no decision. At a little distance stood Vasya. Arkady's heart sank when he looked at him. Vasya was standing, pale, with his head up, stiffly erect, like a recruit before a new officer, with his feet together and his hands held rigidly at his sides. He was looking Yulian Mastakovitch straight in the face. Arkady was noticed at once, and someone who knew that they lodged together mentioned the fact to His Excellency. Arkady was led up to him. He tried to make some answer to the questions put to him, glanced at Yulian Mastakovitch and seeing on his face a look of genuine compassion, began trembling and sobbing like a child. He even did more, he snatched His Excellency's hand and held it to his eyes, wetting it with his tears, so that Yulian Mastakovitch was obliged to draw it hastily away, and waving it in the air, said, 'Come, my dear fellow, come! I see you have a good heart.' Arkady sobbed and turned an imploring look on everyone. It seemed to him that they were all brothers of his dear Vasya, that they were all worried and weeping about him. 'How, how has it happened? how has it happened?' asked Yulian Mastakovitch. 'What has sent him out of his mind?'

'Gra – gra – gratitude!' was all Arkady Ivanovitch could articulate.

Everyone heard his answer with amazement, and it seemed strange and incredible to everyone that a man could go out of his mind from gratitude. Arkady explained as best he could.

'Good Heavens! what a pity!' said Yulian Mastakovitch at last. 'And the work entrusted to him was not important, and not urgent in the least. It was not worth while for a man to kill himself over it! Well, take him away!' . . . At this point Yulian Mastakovitch turned to Arkady Ivanovitch again, and began questioning him once more. 'He begs,' he said, pointing to Vasya, 'that some girl should not be told of this. Who is she – his betrothed, I suppose?'

Arkady began to explain. Meanwhile Vasya seemed to be thinking of something, as though he were straining his memory to the utmost to recall some important, necessary matter, which was particularly wanted at this moment. From time to time he looked round with a distressed face, as though hoping someone would remind him of what he had forgotten. He fastened his eyes on Arkady. All of a sudden there was a gleam of hope in his eyes; he moved with the left leg forward, took three st eps as smartly as he could, clicking with his right boot as soldiers do when they move forward at the call from their officer. Everyone was waiting to see what would happen.

'I have a physical defect and am small and weak, and I am not fit for military service, Your Excellency,' he said abruptly.

At that everyone in the room felt a pang at his heart, and firm as was Yulian Mastakovitch's character, tears trickled from his eyes.

'Take him away,' he said, with a wave of his hands.

'Present!' said Vasya in an undertone; he wheeled round to the left and marched out of the room. All who were interested in his fate followed him out. Arkady pushed his way out behind the others. They made Vasya sit down in the waiting-room till the carriage came which had been ordered to take him to the hospital. He sat down in silence and seemed in great anxiety. He nodded to any one he recognised as though saying goodbye. He looked round towards the door every minute, and prepared himself to set off when he should be told it was time. People crowded in a close circle round him; they were all shaking their heads and lamenting. Many of them were much impressed by his story, which had suddenly become known. Some discussed his illness, while others expressed their pity and high opinion of Vasya, saying that he was such a quiet, modest young man, that he had been so promising; people described what efforts he had made to learn, how eager he was for knowledge, how he had worked to educate himself. 'He had risen by his own efforts from a humble position,' someone observed. They spoke with emotion of His Excellency's affection for him. Some of them fell to explaining why Vasya was possessed by the idea that he was being sent for a soldier, because he had not finished his work. They said that the poor fellow had so lately belonged to the class liable for military service and had only received his first grade through the good offices of Yulian Mastakovitch, who had had the cleverness to discover his talent, his docility, and the rare mildness of his disposition. In fact, there was a great number of views and theories.

A very short fellow-clerk of Vasya's was conspicuous as being particularly distressed. He was not very young, probably about thirty. He was pale as a sheet, trembling all over and smiling queerly, perhaps because any scandalous affair or terrible scene both frightens, and at the same time somewhat rejoices the outside spectator. He kept running round the circle that surrounded Vasya, and as he was so short, stood on tiptoe and caught at the button of everyone – that is, of those with whom he felt entitled to take such a liberty – and kept saying that he knew how it had all happened, that it was not so simple, but a very important matter, that it couldn't be left without further inquiry; then stood on tiptoe again, whispered in someone's ear, nodded his head again two or three times, and ran round again. At last everything was over. The porter made his appearance, and an attendant from the hospital went up to Vasya and told him it was time to start. Vasya jumped up in a flutter and went with them, looking about him. He was looking about for someone.

'Vasya, Vasya!' cried Arkady Ivanovitch, sobbing. Vasya stopped, and Arkady squeezed his way up to him. They flung themselves into each other's arms in a last bitter embrace. It was sad to see them. What monstrous calamity was wringing the tears from their eyes! What were they weeping for? What was their trouble? Why did they not understand one another?

'Here, here, take it! Take care of it,' said Shumkov, thrusting a paper of some kind into Arkady's hand. 'They will take it away from me. Bring it me later on; bring it . . . take care of it . . .' Vasya could not finish, they called to him. He ran hurriedly downstairs, nodding to everyone, saying goodbye to everyone. There was despair in his face. At last he was put in the carriage and taken away. Arkady made haste to open the paper: it was Liza's curl of black hair, from which Vasya had never parted. Hot tears gushed from Arkady's eyes: oh, poor Liza!

When office hours were over, he went to the Artemyevs'. There is no need to describe what happened there! Even Petya, little Petya, though he could not quite understand what had happened to dear Vasya, went into a corner, hid his face in his little hands, and sobbed in the fullness of his childish heart. It was quite dusk when Arkady returned home. When he reached the Neva he stood still for a minute and turned a keen glance up the river into the smoky frozen thickness of the distance, which was suddenly flushed crimson with the last purple and blood-red glow of sunset, still smouldering on the misty horizon . . . Night lay over the city, and the wide plain of the Neva, swollen with frozen snow, was shining in the last gleams of the sun with myriads of sparks of gleaming hoar frost. There was a frost of twenty degrees. A cloud of frozen steam hung about the overdriven horses and the hurrying people. The condensed atmosphere quivered at the slightest sound, and from all the roofs on both sides of the river, columns of smoke rose up like giants and floated across the cold sky, intertwining and untwining as they went, so that it seemed new buildings were rising up above the old, a new town was taking shape in the air . . . It seemed as if all that world, with all its inhabitants, strong and weak, with all their habitations, the refuges of the poor, or the gilded palaces for the comfort of the powerful of this world was at that twilight hour like a fantastic vision of fairyland, like a dream which in its turn would vanish and pass away like vapour into the dark blue sky. A strange thought came to poor Vasya's forlorn friend. He started, and his heart seemed at that instant flooded with a hot rush of blood kindled by a powerful, overwhelming sensation he had never known before. He seemed only now to understand all the trouble, and to know why his poor Vasya had gone out of his mind, unable to bear his happiness. His lips twitched, his eyes lighted up, he turned pale, and as it were had a clear vision into something new.

He became gloomy and depressed, and lost all his gaiety. His old lodging grew hateful to him — he took a new room. He did not care to visit the Artemyevs, and indeed he could not. Two years later he met Lizanka in church. She was by then married; beside her walked a wet nurse with a tiny baby. They greeted each other, and for a long time avoided all mention of the past. Liza said that, thank God, she was happy, that she was not badly off, that her husband was a kind man and that she was fond of him . . . But suddenly in the middle of a sentence her eyes filled with tears, her voice failed, she turned away, and bowed down to the church pavement to hide her grief.

Brief ENCOUNTERS
Short books. *Timeless stories.*

Louisa May Alcott
Behind a Mask

Angela Carter
A Souvenir of Japan

Margery Allingham
The Case of the Late Pig

Vera Caspary
Laura

Margaret Atwood
Significant Moments

Eileen Chang
Young at the Time

Jane Austen
Lady Susan

Colette
The Cat

J. G. Ballard
Venus Smiles

Arthur Conan Doyle
The Parasite

Simone de Beauvoir
Woman of Genius

Anita Desai
Fire on the Mountain

Ingmar Bergman
Sunday's Children

Charles Dickens and Wilkie Collins
The Lazy Tour of Two Idle Apprentices

Roberto Bolaño
Distant Star

Fyodor Dostoevsky
A Gentle Spirit and A Faint Heart

Jorge Luis Borges
The Book of Imaginary Beings

Fumiko Enchi
Masks

Richard Brautigan
In Watermelon Sugar

F. Scott Fitzgerald
The Curious Case of Benjamin Button

Mikhail Bulgakov
The Fatal Eggs

Graham Greene
The Third Man

Toni Cade Bambara
First Light

Jacqueline Harpman
We Were Forbidden

Italo Calvino
The Castle of Crossed Destinies

Ernest Hemingway
The Old Man and the Sea